FORBIDDEN

Eve Bunting

CLARION BOOKS   Houghton Mifflin Harcourt

BOSTON   NEW YORK

Special thanks to Professor Andrea Karlin

Clarion Books

3 Park Avenue

New York, New York 10016

Copyright © 2015 by Edward D. Bunting and Anne E. Bunting Family Trust

All rights reserved. For information about permission to reproduce selections from this book,

write to trade.permissions@hmhco.com or to Permissions, Houghton Mifflin Harcourt

Publishing Company, 3 Park Avenue, 19th floor, New York, New York 10016.

Clarion Books is an imprint of Houghton Mifflin Harcourt Publishing Company.

www.hmhco.com

The text was set in 13 pt. Perpetua Std

LIBRARY OF CONGRESS CATALOGING-IN-PUBLICATION DATA

Bunting, Eve, 1928–

Forbidden / Eve Bunting.

pages cm

Summary: "In early 19th century England, Josie, 16, finds herself in a sinister place with
mysterious, hostile people, including her own relatives. Persistence and determination drive
her to uncover the town's horrifying secret—a conspiracy to wreck and plunder ships—despite
obstacles natural and supernatural."—Provided by publisher.

ISBN 978-0-544-39092-8 (hardcover)

[1. Conspiracies—Fiction. 2. Supernatural—Fiction. 3. Orphans—Fiction.] I. Title.

PZ7.B91527Fp 2015

[Fic]—dc23

2014043063

Manufactured in the United States of America

DOC 10 9 8 7 6 5 4 3 2 1

4500563956

To Christine Bunting and
Richard Wohlfeiler

CHAPTER ONE

WE HAD ARRIVED.

I'd taken two traps, a coach, and a carriage to get here from my old, beloved home in Edinburgh. It was sad and strange to think of myself as an orphan now that my parents had died. But that was what I was. Sorrow threatened to overwhelm me. But I told myself to be brave and to consider myself fortunate to have an aunt and uncle to go to. Though an orphan, I would have a family again.

We'd traveled through wind and rain that grew fiercer the closer we got to the coast. The journey had been tiring and difficult. And then there'd been the strangeness of the last village we'd gone through, where all the shops and houses were brightly lit, people stood around the street, music played loudly through the open doors of one of the establishments. It had seemed to me at first to be filled with gaiety. But only at first. There was a wrongness about it.

Robert, the carriage driver, rushed through it fast, the collar of his greatcoat half hiding his face, his gaze fixed on the road. The carriage bounced and shook so that I feared a wheel might come loose.

When he slowed to avoid a woman singing in the street, I'd gazed at the people around us. They had paused in their conversations and were staring at our carriage, staring at me, with such malevolence that my blood chilled. One man wearing a stained hat shouted, "What's your business here?" in a truculent voice.

A woman yelled, "Go back where you've come from!"

Robert cracked his whip, and we were rattling away, the carriage swaying from side to side.

"This is Brindle?" I'd shouted up to him.

"It is, Mistress."

"The people do not seem friendly," I shouted, holding on to my bonnet to keep it from being blown away. I was going to Brindle Point, a more distant part of the town. Perhaps it would be better.

I'd thought Robert was not going to speak but then he shouted, "I do not know the people here, Mistress. I don't come this way often." He'd muttered something else, but I could not distinguish the words.

The wind had risen to a roar, shaking the sides of the carriage, flailing against the windows. It was difficult to make myself heard as I tried to communicate with him.

"How far now to my uncle's house?"

"No more than a mile, Mistress. Maybe more or maybe less. I'm not from around here."

We were quiet then, rolling unevenly on a road that seemed to grow steadily more narrow. Now and then, I heard the horses whinny, and I wondered about them. Could they see through the dark and wind? Were they exhausted? They needed to rest.

But now Robert was reining them in and the carriage was rumbling to a stop. He helped me to the ground, and I stared in dismay.

"This is the house?"

"It is, Mistress." He tied the strings on his hat more tightly and wrapped his greatcoat more closely around himself before he lifted out my two boxes and my trunk and set them beside me. "If you're sure you want to stay," he said.

What was the matter with him? He had become jittery,

casting anxious looks about him, hurrying in a way that told me he was eager to be off. Certainly the surroundings were not inviting. There was heather with no bloom on it, beaten a brickly brown. There was scrub grass, a tree snarled and crooked, bare rocky ground, clouds that hung low and menacing.

The rain had stopped falling, but the sky was still full of it.

"If that's all, Mistress, I'll be on my way," Robert said.

I could scarcely hear him, for along with the roar and snarl of the wind, there was a boom of waves in the sea below us.

"Wait," I shouted. "You are sure this is Brindle Point? And this is the house of my uncle, Caleb Ferguson?"

"It is, Mistress Josie. I made inquiries at the inn. See the name on the doorpost? Raven's Roost?"

There was no hanging lamp at the door, but when I peered closely, I could make out the name and a date carved into the piece of plank: RAVEN'S ROOST 1707. The house had been there for exactly one hundred years. The board swung in the wind, banging itself against the door that was heavy and studded with nails, not at all in keeping with a house that I could already tell was battered and run-down.

A heavy bell hung on a rope beside it. When I looked up, I saw smoke twisting from the top of a chimney.

"But . . . but . . . my uncle is a professional man," I shouted. "We passed the town a mile back."

"Be that as it may, Mistress. This is his house. I'll clang the bell for you, if you like, and then I'll be off." His soft Scottish burr blurred the words, and the force of the wind blew them away from me. He put a hand on my shoulder. "I was loath to bring you. And you can choose to turn around and come back with me. I'll find you rooms—"

"Thank you," I shouted. "That is kind of you." My hair came loose from my bonnet, which, heaven knew how, was still on my head. I tried to push the long brown curls underneath it. "If I went back, what would I do then?" I held out my hand for him to shake. "Thank you, Robert. You have already been paid for taking me on this long trip?"

"Aye, Mistress. Your solicitor arranged all that. Would you no' write to him and tell him you cannot stay and—"

The door behind us opened. Heat and smoke and light surged out. "I thought I heard you," the man in the doorway said. "You'll be Josie." He addressed Robert. "Bring the lady's valises inside and be quick about it. Is that her trunk? Make haste with it. The cold is perishing."

"I can take the portmanteau . . ." I began, but the man,

who I surmised was my uncle Caleb, said, "Let him do it and be on his way." He walked ahead of me into the house.

For a time I could not get my bearings. The room was a blur, and I had to support myself with a hand on the wall. Behind me I heard the scuffle of Robert's feet as he brought in my belongings. I heard the slide of my trunk being dragged across the lintel. I blinked hard. The smoke in the room was like a fog that stung my eyes and my throat. A woman in a plain black pinafore sat close to a fire that burned in an open hearth. Smoke billowed from it into the room. A steaming pot hung low over the flames. I stood uncertain.

"Here's your niece, Minnie, come all this way to visit us," my uncle said.

The woman was tall and bony, bent at the back as if used to standing under too low a roof. Her gray hair was fixed in a straggly bun. She moved toward me, and I held out my hand. My dear mother had always told me that ladies curtsy and men shake hands, but I could never bring myself to do that. Even though *Mrs. Chandler's Book on Etiquette for Young Ladies* was strict on the subject.

My aunt did not take the hand I offered, merely stepped back. Her eyes were a glittering golden brown, small and hard as brandy-ball sweets. She was examining me the way a man examines a horse he's thinking to buy.

"Mistress Josie?" That was Robert's voice. I turned and saw him standing by my trunk, and I went toward him.

"Don't forget," he muttered. "My wife and I are in Glenbrae, eighteen miles back. Ask anyone the way. But be sure not to tell them you are niece to Caleb Ferguson."

"Thank you, Robert. Thank you for your kindness."

"Why are you standing blathering, man?" my uncle called out. "Are you expecting to be paid more money for your trouble? You're not getting a penny farthing, for I'm sure that solicitor paid you handsomely for your duties."

"He did, thankee." Robert's voice was polite. A crash of wind took the door when he opened it to leave and slammed it shut behind him.

Never in my sixteen years had I felt so desolate. And so alone.

I listened to hear the carriage roll away, but I could hear nothing save the whip of the wind in the chimney, the force of it beating against the outside walls. And the crash of the sea.

"So. You've arrived," my uncle Caleb said, and I looked at him properly for the first time.

He was tall, too, and straight, clean-shaven. His eyes were dark and close set and his dun-colored hair was tied back with a frayed ribbon. There was something about his ears that drew my eyes, though I tried not to stare. They were badly formed, protruding from his head and covered with white scabs, like small hard pearls.

He gave me a smile that had no warmth in it. "You see a resemblance to Duncan?" he asked. "Your late father?"

"No," I whispered, unable to speak more.

"People did say we looked alike when we were bairns, but as you know, he was the elder by a year. We were close in age. But not, I fear, in disposition."

My aunt Minnie gave a snort. My attention swiveled to her and then back to my uncle.

"And then there were these." My uncle paid no mind to her. He raised both hands to cup his ears as if he were hard of hearing. "A strange skin condition that afflicted me at an early age. I venture to say it ruined my life. There is no cure. Stare at them if you want. You must take me as you find me."

"Of course." I tried to smile. No point in saying I hadn't noticed. A person would have to be blind or in the dark not to see what was there.

"Take off your cloak and bonnet, then," my aunt Minnie said. "I've made a stew." Her words were strong and deep, with a coarseness to them that one would not expect from a woman.

I laid my heavy cloak and my bonnet on a high-backed chair.

My uncle indicated a table that almost filled the entire living space. It was oaken, carved at the edges with a design of leaves and fruits, the thick legs ending in clawed feet. It was set with wooden bowls and spoons that shone like silver.

"Be quick with the victuals, Minnie," he called. "The lass is hungry."

"Thank you," I said politely. "There is no need for haste on my account. The coach driver and I ate at the inn before we made this last leg of the journey. But the stew does smell delicious," I added.

"It's ready," my aunt Minnie said.

An oil lamp swung from a hook on the ceiling, and it and the open fire cast light in the room. I saw a fiddle, gleaming chestnut brown on a stool by the fire. My aunt came to the table, took the bowls, and carried them to the hearth. I watched her lift the big iron pot from its swinging arm, set it down, and ladle stew into each bowl. She moved lithely, competently. Before she sat, she took off her pinafore, and I saw that she wore a heavy dark jumper with a faded red ship's wheel on the front of it. And . . . men's rough trousers. I'd never imagined to see a woman in trousers but then I'd never been in the company of a woman like my aunt Minnie before.

I pointed to the violin and in an effort to make

conversation, asked, "You play the instrument, Aunt Minnie?"

"I can make it squawk," she said.

"I can play," I said. "My mother made sure I had music lessons. I could teach you, if you like. Do you have a bow for it?"

She grunted. "I do not want to play it. I just like the looks of it."

"Music lessons!" my uncle muttered. "That is the sort of nonsense Duncan *would* pay good money for."

"My father always did what he thought best for me," I said quickly. "My mother, too. I am grateful."

He and my aunt exchanged glances, and I saw her give a small shake of her head.

I was not only not hungry, I had no appetite whatsoever. I did not care for this criticism of my father, and I decided I would not tolerate it. Perhaps my uncle had been softer and more sensitive when they were prosperous. But, to hear it, there had always been the ears. That in itself could make a man cantankerous.

I surreptitiously gazed around the room. There were signs of wealth and signs of poverty. I quickly decided that my aunt and uncle had come down in the world and lost the apothecary business they had had in Brindle. Perhaps they had once owned a large, fancy house, filled with expensive possessions and had carried some of them with them when they moved.

I lifted my spoon.

"Before we eat, we are accustomed to bless the food," my uncle said sternly.

"Oh." I bowed my head.

"Some hae meat and canna eat, and some can eat and want it," he intoned.

I half opened my eyes and squinted at his face.

It was set in a look of stern piety.

I glanced at my aunt Minnie. Her gaze was fixed on me, her brandy-ball eyes narrowed.

My uncle was continuing with the blessing, and I quickly bowed my head again and tried to look pious myself.

"But we hae meat, and we can eat, so let the Lord be thank-ed." He peered at the two of us. "Amen," he said.

"Amen," my aunt repeated.

I felt an unbecoming levity rise in me as I whispered, "Amen."

My aunt unfurled a stained serviette from a silver serviette ring by her place. Engraved on the ring was the word BONIFACE. It must have been a family name from better times past. She spread the napkin fastidiously across her lap.

Suddenly she asked, "Are you healthy, girl?"

"I . . . I . . ." What an odd question. Almost frightening. "I believe I am," I said. "I did not succumb to the illness that took my dear parents, so I suppose I must be."

"That's good," she said.

I bent my head over the stew. *Are you healthy, girl?* were almost the first words she'd spoken to me. I suddenly thought of the old story of the witch who felt the bones of small, trapped children to see if they were worth cooking in her oven. A shiver trembled across my back. What if Aunt Minnie got up from the table and began poking me, checking to find the fat on me? Asking to see my teeth? Peering down my throat? *Stop it!* I told myself. *Stop these foolish and ghoulish thoughts. There is no comparison. My aunt is simply interested in my well-being. That is all.* And I remembered that it was the witch herself who had ended up in that oven.

CHAPTER TWO

NOW WE CAN PARTAKE of the good food the Lord has provided. With Minnie's help," Uncle Caleb said.

I lifted my spoon.

The fish stew was hearty and warm, and though my morbid thoughts had driven away whatever appetite I had, I managed a mouthful or two. It had herring and potatoes and carrots in it. There was smoke in it, too, but it tasted good. There was no table conversation. From time to time, a thump of wind slapped against the walls, making the house shake. And there was another sound that I could not identify. A higher-pitched whine that shrilled through the whistle of wind. It sounded like a dog.

"Do I hear a dog outside?" I asked. "Perhaps he is lost in the storm."

My aunt continued to spoon her soup, but my uncle said, "It is only Lamb, Minnie's dog. He is locked in the shed for now."

"He does not take kindly to strangers," Aunt Minnie said. "We want to prepare him for you."

"And you for him," my uncle added.

"I am accustomed to a dog," I said. "We had a family spaniel for many years. His name was Ginger."

The thought of Ginger sleeping by our fire, my father reading the paper, my mother at her needlework, brought tears to my eyes. I squeezed them away.

"Lamb is not a family spaniel!" Aunt Minnie bent her head over the food, and I could see that this subject was now closed.

When we had eaten our fill, Uncle Caleb pushed back his chair. "Now I must speak to you of your parents. I should have sent you our condolences at the time of their deaths. That I did not is my shame, and I trust you will forgive me. We offer our condolences now. Influenza, was it not?"

"Yes," I said. "They died two days apart." I tried hard

not to look at his ears as I answered him. It was difficult. Why didn't he cover them with a cap? Or let his hair fall over them? The little beadlike growths shone silvery in the lamplight.

He leaned toward me, and there was something in his eyes I could not put a name to.

"And your parents' house?" he asked. "What became of it?"

"It awaits me," I told them. "There is also the trust, money that I will acquire when I am eighteen. In two years," I added. "I advised Mr. Brougham, my solicitor, that I could live in our home still. I could have a woman come stay with me. I would have been content, and I would not have been a burden to you and Aunt Minnie. But he would have none of it. He would follow my father's wishes." I had such a longing then to be back, for a return to those days of happiness and the warmth of my parents' arms.

I will not weep, I told myself. *I will weep later and let the heartache come.*

Aunt Minnie made a small sound that might have been a sigh. Of sympathy? Of impatience?

"Two years empty? 'Twon't be up to much when you get it."

I made no reply.

Uncle Caleb sat back in his chair. "The solicitor was

quite right. You are no burden. I am sure you are aware that my brother, your father, made the arrangements for you to come to us long ago. Should anything happen to them."

"Yes," I said, and almost added, *Why else do you think I'm here?*

But I didn't need to recall Mrs. Chandler's advice to young ladies to realize that such a remark would be rude and entirely inappropriate. They had taken me in. I would try to be appreciative. I must not make early judgments.

"We are your only relatives, and your father rightly understood that blood is thicker than water. So you are welcome to be with us for the next two years. My brother and I had not seen each other for the past seventeen years, since before you were born. We have communicated. I had advised him of my successful station in life, my apothecary shop, my splendid house in the town here. He no doubt did not know of my new circumstances. Or that my previous wife, Henrietta, had died and that I had remarried."

So my father had thought he was sending me into a comfortable situation.

My uncle removed a silver snuffbox from his waist-coat pocket and partook of a pinch. Aunt Minnie suddenly banged her spoon against the edge of her bowl, and my uncle gave a start. "Oh, forgive me, my dear," he said and passed the snuffbox to her.

I watched her skillfully take a pinch, and almost nothing that had been said or transpired surprised me as much. A woman helping herself to snuff!

What would Mrs. Chandler have to say about that in her etiquette book?

I sat thinking of my poor, ill-informed father, not giving a thought to the possibilities of a change in his brother's circumstances. And never dreaming that he and my mother would die so soon and together.

"I have a new profession now," my uncle said, his nose twitching before he gave forth with a gigantic sneeze. My aunt's sneeze echoed his.

"The work I do now is more to my liking. I believe it was when your solicitor received the information on our change of living styles that he made financial arrangements for me to keep you. You may as well know. We are to receive two guineas a month for your keep and another one hundred guineas from your trust inheritance at the end of two years." He frowned. "To leave behind him money like that, my brother must have been rich. He was the lucky one. I always got the short end of the stick."

My aunt spoke quietly, in a remonstrating tone. "We

must be thankful for the two guineas, Caleb. And we must take care of our dear niece in expectation of more when she leaves us." The words were puzzling and not said in a gracious way. Why did I think of them as menacing? *No need,* I told myself. *It is good that she is speaking at all.*

"True!" They exchanged nods.

"I am a fisherman now," my uncle said. "I have a sturdy boat and the gifts God gives me from the sea. We live a godly life, appreciating His blessings." He pushed back his chair. "Minnie, will you show her where she is to sleep? I fear that carriage driver did not fulfill his obligations and take her belongings where they are to be. You will both have to help me."

I got up from the table, ready to help with the trunk, but my aunt said, "Bring the lamp. I have handled heavier than this. Caleb. Bring the boxes. Go ahead of us, lass."

She picked up the trunk as if it were empty and weighed nothing.

I went ahead, up the narrow stairs, holding the lamp high, their shadows coming after me along the wall.

"That door," she said.

I opened the door she indicated. It was so close to the top stair that I could take one step and be inside it.

She set the trunk on the bare wood floor. Light from the lamp danced across a narrow bedstead made of planks, a small table, a chair, and an ornate chest of drawers. I had a moment to think that it must have also come from their previous home.

"We've made it comfortable for you," Uncle Caleb said. "Your aunt put that quilt on your bed."

"That was kind of you. Did you stitch it yourself?" I asked. It was a pretty bedcover with squares of pink roses and green leaves.

"No. I found it. I'm not a roses kind of woman." She gave a yelp of laughter.

"Thank you for letting me use it," I said.

She did not respond but took a stub of candle from a small drawer in the chest and lit it.

Uncle Caleb lifted the oil lamp and pointed to a row of pegs on the wall. "You can hang your clothes there. Come down again for reading and prayers before you go to your bed. And don't dilly-dally. Your aunt and I believe in early sleep."

I didn't care for being ordered. I didn't want to go down again. But I was there for two years, and I would have to get used to their ways. I would do as he asked — no, demanded — and I must learn not to take umbrage at an autocratic tone of voice.

When they had left, I studied the room. It had a sloping ceiling and one window set high. When I stood on the bed,

I could see through the glass, though there was nothing out there but the dark and one of the twisted limbs of the tree. There was a wooden stool with a basin on it. I could not imagine what purpose the basin had, as there was no water jug to go with it. Perhaps I was supposed to fill one and carry it up so I could wash in private.

I set about putting my undergarments in the dresser drawers and, beneath them, my purse with the small amount of money I'd been given by the solicitor. The books I'd brought, *The Pilgrim's Progress,* a novel by Maria Edgeworth, and two books of poetry, I placed on top of the dresser. I hung my dresses and skirts and my one jacket on the pegs and laid my red shawl on top of my empty trunk. *One day I will put all my belongings back in this trunk, and I will leave Raven's Roost and go home again,* I comforted myself. *I will bring flowers to the graveyard where my dear parents lie, and I will be close to them again.*

Already the room was cold. The sound of the wind shivered the walls as if trying to lift the house and carry us all away. But I reminded myself that it had stood for a hundred years, and it had survived.

Reluctantly I took the candle and went again down the narrow stairs.

My uncle sat at the table, a large Bible in front of him. My aunt, ramrod straight, was opposite him. She motioned to the chair I had sat in to eat my stew. I was distracted by a heavy silver candlestick with three red candles that now adorned the center of the table. And even more distracted by the way my uncle ran his fingers up and down the strange outgrowths on his ears.

He began to read.

"I have heard thy prayer and thy supplication that thou has made before me: I have hallowed this house, which thou hast built, to put my name there for ever."

I listened as he read on. The Bible words always thrilled me, the poetry of them, the sense of antiquity. He read from the Old Testament, and I had no trouble paying attention. It warmed me to think of him and Aunt Minnie as God-fearing. When the reading was over, we knelt at our chairs and my aunt Minnie prayed aloud. Her harsh voice commanded the Lord to look after us and keep us safe in all our endeavors. As an afterthought, she thanked Him for His blessings. She ended by saying, "Help us teach this girl obedience and to not question our ways, or Yours."

I fluttered my eyes open and saw that she was watching me again. It was as if she was talking to me and not to God.

In the moment of silence that followed her prayer, the dog gave a high, piercing whine.

"Be quiet, Lamb!" my aunt muttered, and the whine cut off instantly.

The dog was outside in a shed. Had he heard her voice through the walls and through the clamor of the storm? I had always known that dogs had acute hearing. But was this possible?

We said our amens and rose to our feet.

My uncle leaned across the table and extinguished the candles with a silver snuffer.

"The Three in One," he said. "The Father, the Son, and the Holy Ghost. You know your Scriptures, I hope?"

I nodded.

"Get you to bed now." He turned away from me.

There was to be no good-night embrace as there had always been from my mother, no kiss on the cheek as there had been from my father. No "sleep well, dearest." Nothing.

These were their manners, and I was not to question.

"Good night," I told them and picked up my candle.

"Good night, girl."

I started up the stairs. But I had forgotten my cloak and bonnet that I'd draped on the chair when I first entered Raven's Roost. I went down again, quietly, to retrieve them.

My uncle was speaking. "Will she be strong enough, Minnie?" he asked.

"In body, yes. In her head, I do not know," my aunt answered. "We may have to persuade her."

There was a silence. I clutched the banister, afraid to move. Then my aunt said, "Archie sent a message. There's a goodly one on its way. He's been riding along the shore path, keeping an eye on it. He says in all likelihood it'll be here tomorrow. Praise be that it's not tonight and her just arrived. We'll have time to make arrangements afore it gets here."

"Aye," my uncle agreed. "I feel in my bones it will be worth the wait. She's young and strong. She'll be choice."

I left my cloak and bonnet where they were and went silently back to my room.

CHAPTER THREE

I WAS TIRED, but I was unable to sleep. What did they mean by "choice"? It seemed to refer to my youth and strength. To aid them in the fishing? To help my aunt Minnie in the house? That puzzle, along with the unknown noises and the turmoil of my thoughts, kept me awake. What a strange pair they were, this aunt and uncle. They talked in conundrums. Would I ever be at ease with them? I buried my head in the pillow that smelled of dried leaves and fought my feelings of despair. My hopes that I would have a family, that my aunt and uncle would be soft and loving had been wiped away.

The walls thrummed with the force of the wind, as if it was trying to get in. The ocean roared and raged, booming in my ears. I could hear the surge and suck of it as the waves advanced and crashed on rocks so regularly that I began to time them. Six seconds, the noise getting louder, the crash, the hissing, a long-drawn-out rattling like a stick pulled along a fence, the momentary silence, and then the pattern starting again.

How unfamiliar it all was. Almost frightening.

I got out from under the quilt and climbed on the bed to look again through the window; there was still nothing to see but the clouded dark and an occasional flash of white somewhere far below. It must be the curling of a wave. We were on a cliff, I knew, and the sea filled the space below, the Atlantic, roaring in to smash this northernmost coast of Scotland. My solicitor had shown me Brindle on the map. *I am surprised it is even marked,* he'd said. *I understand it is very small but probably beautiful, in a wild way. Your uncle's home is on Brindle Point, a mile from the town.*

I'd nodded. At that time, I did not care where I would be living. I knew only that I had no home, no parents. Now I had seen Brindle. And it had not looked beautiful.

I'd snuffed my candle long since, but as my eyes grew more accustomed to the dark, I could see the shape of my clothes on the pegs, like mad people swaying to the beat of the sea. There was my white muslin dress in the new Empire style. My mother's seamstress had made it for me. It was to be worn to the Brailey Ball but now, unused by me, it danced to the ocean's calling. The dress was transparent. I knew that some of the more daring, sophisticated women had taken to wearing one such without a shift below it, a style popular in France. It was rumored that some of the highborn ladies there appeared in public with bare breasts. I could not fathom this. The seamstress had provided a shift to go under mine. It was a beautiful dress, soft and flowing, and swirled when I walked. My mother had given me her opal brooch to wear at the neck. "My darling Josie," she'd said. "Do you know how proud your father and I are of you? Do you know how dearly we love you?"

Four days later, they were both dead.

Sobs that I could no longer contain tore at my chest and throat. I got out of bed again, found the brooch where she'd fastened it, and pinned it on my nightgown, then folded my hand over it and tried once more to sleep.

I dozed, but I wakened fully to a *plop, plop, plop.*

Disoriented, I could not for a moment think where I could be.

Plop, plop, plop.

I was here, destined to live for two whole years with my strange aunt and uncle.

Plop, plop, plop.

I fumbled for the candle and lit it.

Immediately I saw the cause of the sound. Rain slashed against the high window and fell, drop by drop, from the ceiling into the basin, which, I now realized, had been placed suitably on the stool. When I looked up, I saw a chink in the roof. The basin was half full. What if it overflowed? That would not be a good beginning for my stay in Raven's Roost. I sat on the bed, the quilt draped around me, watching it, watching how quickly it fell. It was going to slop over unless the rainstorm ceased. I'd have to find a larger receptacle.

Shivering with cold, I took my red shawl, wrapped it about me to cover my nightgown, and opened my door. Close by, I heard loud snores coming from the room next to mine. Which of them was it, making that frightful noise?

I went quickly down the stairs. Somewhere there must be a pot, the one the stew had been in or another, larger. There might be a bucket.

The candle was only a stub. I had to hurry before it went out. I was on the bottom step of the stairs when I heard it. A low rumble, the kind that comes from an animal's throat when it is about to attack. What was it? Dear heaven!

I turned quickly, stumbling on the hem of my nightgown, tripping over the droop of my shawl, which had slipped from my shoulders, my only frantic thought to get back up the stairs and behind my closed door. But I was not quick enough.

The candle fell from my hand, went out, and in the darkness, I felt the savage grip of teeth on my ankle and that fierce, low growl that made my heart go cold.

"Uncle Caleb," I screamed. "Help!"

What was it? It had to be the dog!

I tried to tug my foot away, but the slightest movement sent a shard of sharp pain along my ankle and caused the growling to intensify and the teeth to clamp even more tightly.

Perspiration broke out on me. I told myself to stay absolutely still, but instinct took over. I tried once more to free myself and felt the teeth tear across the top of my foot, then dig even deeper into my skin. I held myself stiff. What if he decided to let go of my foot and tear at my throat?

There was the merciful sound of movement above and

then the faint glow of a candle and my aunt's voice: "Lamb! Leave her be!"

Instantaneously, the teeth snapped open, and I whimpered and tried to sit on the stair. In the light from the candle, I saw slobber and blood on my ankle and foot and on the hem of my nightgown. I groaned.

My aunt stepped over me, not even inquiring if I'd been injured or needed attention. "It's only Lamb," she said.

A yellow glow filled the living room as she lit the oil lamp and I saw the dog. He was an Alsatian, golden brown. His eyes were fixed on me.

My aunt crouched beside him cooing, "Good dog, Lamb. Good boy, did his duty, so he did."

This was the dog whose name was Lamb? No lamb had ever had such teeth!

My uncle stood on the step behind me. "What were you doing?" he roared. "Sleekiting down here to spy. Well, there'll be no spying in my house. You hear me? Mark that well! You'll find out that Lamb is always on guard."

I dragged myself upright. When I bent over to look, I saw the two semicircles of teeth marks, each one welling with drops of blood.

My uncle stared down at me. "Are ye all right?" he asked at last, his eyes not even on me but on the kitchen below, and it was as if he'd remembered something, some nicety that he'd forgotten and should use.

I gathered my shawl around me, too shaken to try to defend myself against his accusations.

"Minnie," he called, "the lass needs a bit of cloth to tie round her foot. And you," he said to me, "go down and fetch it and then take yourself back to your bed."

"Stay there, Lamb," Minnie told the dog, and he sat, his evil gaze no longer on me but on her. I was afraid to go down the stairs past where he was.

"Come on! He'll no' touch you now since I talked to him," my aunt said. "I told you we had to prepare him. Take a cloth from that pile in the kitchen." She bent down to the dog, whispering to him, stroking his neck, putting her face close to his.

I hobbled cautiously around them, took the top piece of cloth that looked like the tail of a chemise, and hobbled back up the dark stairs.

Plop, plop, plop.

The drops were filling into the basin, and I did not care. Let it overflow. Let it run down the stairs. Let it drown everybody in the house, especially the dog.

I dipped the cloth in the cold water, where bits of debris floated, then bound it round my foot and pulled a stocking over it.

If I'd expected my aunt or uncle to come to my room and inquire about the savage bite, I'd have been wrong. I heard them pad past my door.

Was the dog with them? No. He would still be on guard downstairs. Still. He'd done what he was supposed to do.

He was a good dog.

CHAPTER FOUR

D ESPITE THE THROBBING of my foot and my frightening thoughts, I slept. When I wakened, sun was streaming through the small window high on the wall, and I quickly got out from under the quilt and stood on my bed, favoring my right foot.

The sky was blue. Streaky white clouds feathered across it, and I could see over the sea to the far horizon. The water in the basin was almost to the top. I sat on the bed, took off the stocking and the cloth, and examined the teeth marks. There they were, six red points in an almost complete circle on my ankle and gouges across my foot, all caked with dried blood. I prodded them gently. I did not like it that they were inflamed, but at least they were not suppurating.

I stood in the center of the room then, wondering what to do next.

There was a chamber pot under the bed, and I had need of it. But a fastidiousness that I knew to be ridiculous always stopped me from such a convenience. It was the same now. Somewhere there must be an outhouse or water closet. But what about Lamb? Was he still there, at the bottom of the stair?

I had to go. But this time, I would be prepared.

I got dressed in the plainest gingham dress I'd brought, my thickest stockings and sturdiest shoes. As I tried to pull on the shoe, pain raced through my ankle. I clenched my teeth and persisted, tying the laces loosely. There! I was ready.

But Lamb?

I hobbled to the dresser and searched for something I could use to defend myself. There were two long drawers, where I'd put my folded garments, and eight small ones, possibly for writing paper. In the fourth one down, I found a quill pen, the point sharpened to be keen as a needle. The feathers on it were matted and stuck together, but I was not concerned about penmanship. I weighed it in my hand, point out. Yes. If Lamb came at me, I would stab him. For a moment, I wondered if I would be capable of inflicting such pain. But then I became aware again of the misery in my foot and ankle. I would be capable.

I took a few tentative steps down the stairs.

The house was quiet, smelling still of smoke. There was no sign of my aunt or my uncle, no sound. They had gone out. It was apparent that they cared nothing for me that they would leave me without a word on my first morning. They were obviously not concerned about my wounded foot.

Where was Lamb? Had they taken him with them?

I limped warily down the rest of the stairs, holding the banister, the quill clutched in my other fist, point out.

All was quiet.

Now I could see into the room below. It was very tidy. I saw my cloak and bonnet where I'd left them.

I saw Lamb.

He lay by the door, watching me, his ears upright, his tail moving slowly. Last night, in pain and by candlelight, I had not clearly seen him.

I stopped.

He was huge. He could have been part wolf. His mouth hung half open, and I saw his teeth, pointed, white, and shining. I remembered the feel of those teeth and took a tighter grip on the quill.

Hurriedly, I took a step back.

My breath was coming in short, hurtful gasps.

We were watching each other. I sensed that the wrong move would be disastrous.

I wet my lips. "Lamb," I whispered.

He didn't move.

"Good dog," I murmured.

I took another step down, and another.

I was on the floor now, standing perfectly still. I moved toward him, one small hobble at a time, the quill at the ready.

His gaze was disinterested.

I opened the door quietly, closed it behind me, then leaned against the outside wall, taking deep breaths. He'd let me go.

A ridiculous thought slid into my mind. My aunt Minnie must have instructed him not to touch me this morning, and he had agreed. I shook my head to clear it. As if a person and a dog could have a conversation and an understanding. I must not allow myself to have such ridiculous ideas.

I spread my arms wide.

I was out.

The morning was lovely. September weather in Scotland, storming one day, mild the next. It had been that way in Edinburgh. We would plan a picnic, and suddenly summer would be winter, with a cold wind howling down from the Castle on the Rock, blowing its way along Princes Street, lifting the litter in the gutters, sending it spinning. *Enough, Josie. You must not keep looking back. It is now, and you are here.*

Behind Raven's Roost, I saw the shed that was likely where Lamb had been imprisoned the previous night. I let my gaze drift from the shed to the house. The two buildings were well separated, on either side of a path. But last night he'd heard Minnie's voice. And he had obeyed.

The shed was a more recent structure than Raven's Roost, made of thick boards. No windows in it. Only the door, which I quickly saw was bolted and locked. And, to my relief, there was an upright wooden structure of a size and shape that I knew could only be an outhouse. Inside was unpleasant but serviceable, and I was glad of it.

To the side of the shed was a fenced space with a brown horse grazing on the wild grass. Five chickens pecked in the dirt.

I hobbled to the edge of the cliff and looked over. Below was the sea, calm and blue and shining. Small, happy waves cavorted on the strip of sand. Between the sand and the cliff was a band of shingle, small rocks that sparkled wet where they lay.

There were people on the beach, just a few. A path led down, and I was about to take it when I noticed a pump at the side of the house with a bucket beside it. I'd not had a chance to wash since I came, so I made my way across to it and pumped up some fresh water. All the time, I kept my eye on the house and especially on the door. What if Lamb burst through, having changed his mind about me? Of course he could not open a door. Or could he? I'd slipped the quill into the pocket of my dress, and I reassured myself that it was still there.

I filled the bucket of water, washed my hands and face, and dried them on the hem of my dress. For a moment, I stared at the water, wishing I could plunge my foot into it. But to remove my stocking there, with no privacy, was repugnant.

The path was steep, but there was a handrail. Sandy clumps of heather and coarse grass grew along its sides. I made slow progress, but it was agreeable out in the sun and air. My black fears of the night had eased, and I decided that I had exaggerated every happening. My aunt and uncle were not as I'd thought they would be. They were rougher, less mannered, almost rude, but that was their practice, and circumstances had brought them to it. I would have to thole.

From there I could see fishing boats pulled high on the shore. There were four of them, wooden, each long and wide with an open deck. They were all rigged for two masts, sturdy, strong, and, though weather- and sea-battered, beautiful in their own way. How strange that all were painted in dark colors. Two were black as coal, one gray as fog, one a shadowy dark blue, the color of the sea at night.

The Pentland Firth, this part of the ocean was called. Mr. Brougham, my solicitor, had pointed it out to me on the map.

"This is a dangerous stretch of water," he'd told me in his sonorous voice. "But busy. If a ship does not go through the firth on its way to the continent of Europe, it must go all the way through the English Channel. Most ships take their chances with the firth. There's many a wreck." His finger with its long nail traced the way the ships would sail. His stubby finger moved north. "Thick fogs come down from the north. There be rocks, too, to add to their trouble."

I'd listened politely, too concerned with my own sorrow and fear of the future to pay much attention.

All was peaceful now. In front of me, along the ocean's edge, were small rocks on which seagulls perched. I saw one flat rock, the sea drifting aimlessly around its base, the sun polishing its gray stone, and I limped toward it and sat, feeling for the first time a kind of peace.

There was no one nearby. The figures on the beach were still far away. I glanced around, slipped off my shoe and stocking and pulled the hem of my dress up so that it would not get wet. I'd never felt so daring. The sea drifted over my wounds. Oh, but the water was cold! In a few seconds, my foot was numb, but I held it in place. The sea was pure, the salt that stung the sores would heal them.

I was so startled when a voice spoke behind me that I jerked my foot out of the water, leaving it to dangle. The skirt of my dress rucked up most unbecomingly.

"I'm sorry if I surprised you," the voice said, and I turned as well as I was able to stare up at the young man who'd spoken.

"You did surprise me. I did not think there was anyone near." I pulled down my dress. "It would have been polite to announce your coming. I thought myself alone."

"I came down the path," he said, "and saw you. Please accept my apologies." He sounded half sincere and half mocking.

I bristled, taking stock of him. His hair, black as ebony, was cropped short in a style not at all fashionable. But of course, this was Brindle, not Edinburgh. He might have been handsome, except that his expression was disagreeable. I searched for the word to describe him and decided on *brooding,* as if he carried unbearable secrets. And what was he wearing? The shirt looked like an undergarment, leaving his arms and shoulders bare. His canvas trousers came only to below his knee. I had never seen such attire. He was barefoot.

"I was bathing my foot," I said unnecessarily.

He bent down to look. "A dog bite. Does it pain you?"

"Yes," I said. "But I think the salt water will revive it." I spread my dress more decorously across my leg. I would have to wait till he went away to pull on my stocking.

"The wound needs attention." He touched the skin around it with one finger, and I immediately jerked my foot away.

"Sir!" I said.

"I am sorry. Did I hurt you?"

"It was not that," I said stiffly.

I saw a glimmer of a smile. "If I was too forward in touching you, accept another apology. But I was determining if the bite needs more than salt water to heal. And I believe it does. See the redness spreading? The wound is spoiling."

I gathered my wits about me. "I thank you for your consideration. But I will tell you, I soaked my ankle in cold water immediately. I do not expect any trouble." I had a quick memory of the dirty drips in the washbasin. "And now I have purified it in the ocean," I added. "I am sure it will cure itself."

He was looking at me intently. I had not noticed the color of his eyes. They were blue, and like the opal in the brooch my mother had given me, they seemed to change to an almost green, even as I looked at them. His eyebrows were dark as soot. Perhaps that was what gave him the appearance of a scowl.

"May I help you get up?" he asked.

"Thank you, but I can help myself."

He still stood, then said, "I have not seen you here before. May I ask your name?"

"Josie Ferguson. I am now living at Raven's Roost."

"You are Caleb Ferguson's daughter?" His voice had taken on a different tone.

"No," I said. "I am his niece. I have come to live with him and my aunt for two years."

He nodded, frowned. "You have come at a bad time."

What did he mean? I had already surmised that any time would be bad.

I edged myself sideways along the rock, legs dangling, and set one foot down on the wet sand. I would dearly have loved some help, but I had chosen to refuse it and could no longer ask. I tried to take a step and almost fell over. The numbness had gone from my foot, and it seemed as if a hundred biting insects were feasting on it.

"I would like some privacy, please, while I put on my stocking and shoe," I said stiffly, thinking that a gentleman would have rushed to my aid, no matter what I had previously said.

He turned his back and spoke away from me. "Was it Lamb who bit you?"

"Yes," I said, trying to dry my foot on the hem of my dress, which was wet too. I gave up and pulled my stocking over the dampness. The pressure hurt, and I winced. But it was done. The shoe was impossible.

"You may turn around now," I said.

He looked at me, at my stockinged foot.

"Perhaps if we introduce ourselves properly, you will allow me to help you. I am Eli Stuart."

"As I told you, I am Josie Ferguson."

"I don't think you will be able walk across the shingle unaided, Mistress Ferguson," he began, and I sighed and said, "Oh, please call me Josie."

"It would be sensible to lean on my shoulder, if you are not too timid to touch me," he said.

"Timid? I am not timid in the least. I am merely in a difficult situation." One glance at the uneven shingle, the sharp small stones, and I knew I had no choice. "I have no choice," I said and put my hand and my weight on his shoulder. It would have been less familiar if his shoulder had been covered, but my hand was on warm, smooth skin, and I felt color rise in my face. Almost instantly, I realized how difficult it would be to continue in this posture. He was taller than I, and I could not get the support I needed. I stumbled, and he turned and caught me. Before I could thank him or protest—before I could decide which I wanted to do—he lifted me and carried me over the sand, over the shingle, to where the path began.

I was mortified. At some point, I had felt myself slipping, and I'd put my arms around his neck. How could I have done that? I was shameless. My cheek had been pressed against his shoulder, his bare shoulder.

"You may release me now," I said coldly, and he set me down where the path began. My heart was pounding. I had never been so handled, at least not by a young man. I straightened my wet and wrinkled dress. "Thank you," I muttered grudgingly.

He smiled. It was an amused smile that changed his face, made it almost handsome.

"I was glad to be of assistance," he said.

"I can climb the path without help," I told him. "There is the handrail, and I can take my time."

A woman was coming down the narrow path as I spoke. She wore a dark skirt and a high-necked blouse.

"Good morning, Mrs. Kitteridge," Eli Stuart said.

She stopped, observing us.

"Good morning, Eli." She pointed at me. "Who is this?"

"This is Mistress Josie Ferguson, niece to Mr. and Mrs. Ferguson. She had an unfortunate accident to her ankle. This is Mrs. Kitteridge," he added unnecessarily.

I could not help but notice that she wore a ring on the finger that she pointed. It had a deep red stone that blazed in the sunlight. Then I saw that she had a ring on every finger of each hand, all of them glittering like glass. But I could tell they were not glass. I had seen such gems in the windows of elegant establishments in Edinburgh.

"You'll be helping your aunt and uncle, then?" Mrs. Kitteridge asked.

"Yes," I said.

Beside me, I saw Eli shift.

"They'll be glad of another pair of hands and sharp young eyes," she said.

Sharp young eyes? What meaning was I to take from that?

"We must be going," Eli told her.

She put a beringed hand on his arm. "You must come soon and see Daphne," she purred. "She pines for you."

"I am sure she has more important things to do," Eli said, but I could tell he was discomfited. He stood aside to let Mrs. Kitteridge pass.

She walked away from us toward the sea, her feet crunching in the shingle.

"I would like to suggest something to you," Eli said. "I do not like how that ankle looks. There is poison in it, from the teeth."

Or from the water in the basin, I thought guiltily.

He pointed. "I live with my grandmother in that house you can see among the trees. My grandmother knows herbs and potions and can cure anything, from a cut to a broken leg. I've seen her put a poultice on a festering wound and draw out the corruption. It would pleasure her to help you."

I could not believe it. This young gentleman whom I did not know, not content to have embarrassed me by carrying me in his arms, was proposing that I go with him to his grandmother's house. Unchaperoned. Now.

He was looking at me in a questioning manner. I had no doubt his suggestion had been made out of kindness, and perhaps, here in Brindle, refined manners had disappeared. But to do what he recommended would be impossible for me.

"Thank you," I said. "But my uncle Caleb is an

apothecary with, I am sure, knowledge of cures. I will wait for him to come back and tend to me."

For a moment, I thought about how unconcerned my uncle and aunt had been last night. But this was not something I would reveal to a stranger.

"Oh, yes. Your uncle Caleb." There was that scowl again. "You say you will be helping him? Are you aware of what he does?"

"He is a fisherman," I said.

"Yes. And more. I wish you well, Mistress Josie."

And before I could ask the meaning of his words, he strode away.

CHAPTER FIVE

THE PATH WAS MORE DIFFICULT than I'd thought. I had to stop three times as I pulled myself along. Each time I halted, I looked, half ashamed of my action, for Eli Stuart. I did not see him. Why didn't I dismiss him from my thoughts as I had dismissed his offer of help? I told myself that I dwelled on him merely because the time with him had been so irregular. Having him touch me, having him carry me! He'd smelled of the sea. I was aghast that I could not instantly dispel the vulgar thoughts I was having.

The few people at the other end of the beach were coming this way. They seemed to know one another. They were gesticulating, sometimes slowing to talk.

I hobbled back to the house. When I reached the door, I paused. Where was Lamb? Would he be as permissive as he had been earlier? Would he remember that I was friend to Aunt Minnie? Was the quill still in my pocket?

It was. I took it out and held it at the ready. In my other hand, I clutched my shoes. One would be good as a stout club.

I opened the door an inch. "Lamb?" I called, cajolingly. "It's Josie." I took a deep breath. There I was, talking as if the dog understood, as if he knew my name! That was all right for my aunt Minnie, who I had already decided was slightly strange. But not for me.

Listening, I heard nothing.

I opened the door a little wider and saw Lamb lying in front of the lintel. To get in, I would have to step over him, which I did, holding my breath.

He made no move.

"Good dog," I whispered.

He lifted his head and gazed at me. His tail wagged peacefully.

Whatever he'd been told of me, he remembered.

I edged to the stairs and climbed to my room. The

brimming basin of water was where I had left it. I bent over it. Yes, little bits of roofing that might be a hundred years old floated on top. There was pebbly dirt too, scattered across the bottom. I had been foolish to use it.

The foot of my stocking was wet and sandy. I eased the stocking off and peered closely at my ankle. The redness had spread alarmingly across the top of my foot, and it hurt simply to look at it.

The bite needs more than salt water, Eli with the blue-green eyes had said. The blue-green eyes and the hair black as a crow. I was beginning to think he was right.

Where were my uncle and aunt? On this, my first day, one would have thought they would have stayed with me or at least informed me of their plans. But they had not. I felt a rush of self-pity and pushed it away. There was no need to be childish.

When I went back down, the sitting room was still empty, save for the dog, who appeared oblivious to me. There must be something I could find to dull this pulsating pain. Some salve or unguent. My uncle had been an apothecary, after all. He still was. Wouldn't he have brought some of his medicines with him?

Lamb lifted his head and watched me.

The sharpened quill in my pocket did not reassure me.

But there was a knife on the draining board. I moved it to where I could easily reach it, should the need arise.

When I looked at him again, he had closed his eyes. I breathed more easily.

Shelves were stacked in the kitchen corner. On them were bags of flour and sugar, a drum of salt, cornstarch, treacle, a round of butter sitting in a bowl of water. There was potato bread tied up in a cloth. Carrots and parsnips in a gaping sack underneath.

No salves or balms there.

I took a triangle of potato bread to ease my hunger.

There was one last cupboard, small and undistinguished. It was high above the shelving, out of my reach. I hopped to the nearest chair, one foot raised. It was the chair my aunt Minnie had sat on last night.

Across from me, too close, Lamb moved, and I froze. But he had only stretched sleepily and put his head down again.

It was hard to drag the chair and place it underneath the small, high cupboard. I struggled and got it in place, then hiked my dress up and tucked it into my pantaloons so it would not trip me. I clambered onto the chair, uncertain still if I could reach the cupboard.

A large Toby Jug depicting a scowling pirate with a

dagger in his teeth watched me from the high shelf, as if forbidding me to proceed. I looked away from him and stretched up my arms, my fingers touching a lock.

There was a sudden growl behind me.

I stiffened, arms raised, too afraid to lower them and turn around. I moved my head cautiously and saw Lamb. He was right beneath me, and I stifled a scream as he put both front paws on the chair and stood upright, his mouth no more than a few inches from my bare foot. Standing like this, he was massively tall and terrifying. I could see every little bristling hair on him, each one silver tipped, shading to gold. I could see his teeth and the glistening saliva on his tongue. I had never fainted in my life, and I told myself I was not going to now. I had to be strong.

"Lamb?" I murmured. I tried to speak softly, kindly, but the dryness in my mouth and throat produced only a croak. "It's Josie. Remember? Minnie is my aunt. She likes me."

The low growl was louder now.

I dared not move even slightly. I dared not speak again.

Why had he changed? A few moments ago, he'd been quiet, lazy, not threatening.

When the knock came on the door, my heart soared. Someone! Did I have the courage to shout for help?

I didn't have to.

The door opened, and I saw Eli Stuart.

And at the same time, something inexplicable happened.

Lamb's paws slid down from the chair where I stood numbed with fear, and he slunk, belly down, whimpering instead of growling, and squeezed himself into the corner by the hearth.

I was so stupefied that I swayed and grasped the back of the chair for support.

Eli came toward me.

"You can come down now," he said. "I am here."

I was not about to faint, but I might have been about to cry. Relief flooded me.

He stood by my chair. "Take my hand."

I turned slightly to look at Lamb. He was watching Eli, drooling. Long drips of saliva hung from his bottom lip. And he was whining.

"Are you sure it is safe?" I asked.

"Yes. Lamb knows me."

I was still doubtful.

"Come!"

I reached out my hand, and he took it and helped me to sit and then stand, wavering a little. I kept Eli between me and the dog. His hand was rough and warm and reassuring. I clung to it, all reservations gone.

"Thank you," I said. "Lamb was permissive with me and then he threatened me. I do not know why."

"Perhaps he has been told not to let anyone touch that high cupboard," Eli said.

"What could be in there that needs to be so protected?" I asked.

He released my hand, then took hold of my arm.

There was no point in decorum. I let him guide me to another chair.

He set the one I'd stood on back in its place by the table.

"I was searching for a salve or a balm to soothe the bite," I said. "I am afraid it is contaminated." I cast another nervous look at Lamb, who lay motionless, making strange groaning noises in his throat.

"That is why I came in search of you," Eli said. "I went to my grandmother's house and talked with her. She says you must have the bite seen to at once. I do not wish to frighten you. But she told me of a disease called lockjaw."

"What is that?"

"It is what it sounds like. And it is fatal. You cannot wait for your uncle to return. He and your aunt are out on the Sisters, where they go each day at low tide. They will not come back till much later."

"The Sisters? What are they?" I did not wait for an answer and did not care. I was talking because, now that I was safe from Lamb, I had other worries.

Lockjaw?

"The reef that is uncovered at low tide is called the Sisters." He cupped my foot in his hand and bent over it. "I am instructed by my grandmother to convince you to come to her. At this moment, she is mixing herbs and other potions to spread on the bite and draw out the poison. I have told her I cannot make you come if you resist. But I can advise you."

I retrieved my bare foot. Unthinkable that he had taken hold of it like that. I struggled for a minute between propriety and alarm.

"I will go with you. But I will need to get another stocking and my shoe," I said.

There was that smile again, that dazzle that seemed to me filled with amusement.

"Of course you must go alone," he said. "It would never do for you to be improper."

Was he making mock of me?

"I do not like the tone of your voice," I said, and did not add, *Or the ridicule in your smile,* though I thought it.

"You must excuse me," he said. "I do not have a gentleman's manners. But I will get the stocking for you if you tell me where to find it."

"No. I will fetch it myself." To have this stranger opening one of the drawers where my intimate clothes lay would be embarrassing. And I had no wish to remain in this room, on my own, with Lamb.

He shrugged. "As you wish."

"May I ask why Lamb appears to fear you?" I asked.

Eli moved across the room to where the dog lay, and petted him. He looked up at me. "He senses that I am more formidable than he is."

CHAPTER SIX

I STRUGGLED UP THE NARROW STAIRS. My stockings were in a drawer with my pantaloons and shifts and the stays that I hoped never to wear while I was here. I chose my only black stockings and found that I could, albeit with extreme discomfort, maneuver one of them over my right foot. My decision to go with Eli, however humiliating, was the correct one. It was strange how he described himself as formidable, though Lamb appeared to agree.

I went back downstairs without my shoe, looking first

at Lamb and then at Eli. The dog lay curled in a ball, his paws shielding his eyes.

"What is it that ails him?" I asked. "He looks ill. He cannot still be fearful!"

"He will recover," Eli said.

"I am ready now to go with you," I told him.

We left Raven's Roost and walked side by side through the coarse grass. A nettle, tall and poisonous, stung my hand.

I blew on my skin where a red rash was already beginning.

"Here." Eli pulled a leaf from the plant beside it, raised my hand, and rubbed the leaf on the blisters. I felt relief almost immediately.

"Usually the dock leaf and the nettle grow together," he said. "The harm one does, the other eases."

His face was close to mine. His gaze unnerved me. I forced myself to concentrate on the sting, though it was no longer troubling me.

I seemed to be short of breath.

He released his hold on me.

"You are very pale," he said. "I had wished my grandmother could come to you, but she told me she had to be by her own fire and have her own ingredients to hand."

"It is very kind of her to see me at all," I said.

I was having trouble walking. It was humpity underfoot, and the holes in the grass caught my shoe, jerking me enough one time to make me yelp.

"May I carry you again?"

I looked for that mockery and ridicule in his voice but did not hear it. I stopped, facing him, feeling the dampness of sweat on my forehead.

"It would be easier on me," I said. "But I fear the unseemliness of it would distress me. Think me foolish, if you will. But I will persevere."

He shrugged.

"I will, however, hold on to your arm again," I added.

Without another word, he proffered his arm, his bare arm, sun-warmed and smooth, and I clasped it, wondering briefly what Mrs. Chandler would have to say if she could see me.

We spoke little on the way to his grandmother's house. I was busy with my thoughts and with my attempt not to show the pain that came with each step I took.

Why had Lamb been afraid of Eli? I pondered this as we walked side by side across stubble and through the wild heather. Had Eli once ill-used the dog? Had he kicked him? Tormented him? Could that have been what he meant when he'd said he was "formidable"?

None of this seemed in keeping with what I had seen of Eli.

But who knew what could be hidden under a handsome exterior?

There was something else bothering me. Why was I so discomfited by his presence? Why did I feel heat rise in me when I allowed myself to glance up at him? Was I just a silly female, dithery in the presence of a comely young man? I must work on suppressing that at once.

"We are here," he said.

The house was small, much smaller than Raven's Roost, with only one story. Roses climbed around the lintel. Seashells lined the path that led to the door, and Eli let go of my hand, stooped, and righted one of the shells that had been moved out of place.

"I collected all these when I was a bairn," he said. "I carried them in a wee red pail and arranged them." He looked up at me and smiled. For a moment, I saw the little boy struggling up the hill with his red pail filled with shells for his grandmother, and my heartbeat quickened. I wished I had known him then.

"Excuse me," he said and stepped ahead of me to open the door.

The room inside was filled with light from small open windows.

I don't know what I expected Eli's grandmother to be, but she was, to me, unexpected. Small and round with hair as black as her grandson's and a cheerful expression. She looked so much more pleasant than my aunt Minnie or Mrs. Kitteridge.

She walked quickly toward me and said, "I am Eli's grandmother, Doss Stuart. I am so glad you came. When Eli described the bite to me, I knew you must let me tend to it."

She indicated a chair by a small table. "May I see your foot?"

The table held a large wooden bowl and several smaller ones in which I saw collections of different leaves and flowers. There were small bottles part filled with liquids.

"Thank you for your concern," I said. "I trust this is not too much trouble?"

She smiled. "Not at all, my dear."

Eli was hovering behind me. "I will be at my work," he said. "Knock if you need me."

I was glad he'd gone without my having to request it. But what work was he going to?

He strode out the door and closed it behind him.

"Do you want me to help you?" Doss Stuart knelt beside me, looking up at me with bright, dark eyes.

"I think I can manage." I removed my garter and rolled

down my stocking. The foot of it was stuck fast to the wound. I gritted my teeth, closed my eyes, and pulled it free.

"Oh, my, yes," she said. "We need to take care of this. It was Lamb, was it not? He can be vicious. The punctures are deep. And see? You must have tried to pull away, because the skin is ripped."

"I may have. I do not rightly remember."

"I am not surprised. There is something pernicious in a dog's saliva. You have heard of lockjaw?"

"Not until Eli made me aware of it."

"The jaw is locked closed because of a spasm in the muscles. You would be unable to speak. Or eat. But we have started on treatment quickly. I do not believe you need to worry."

"I thank you from the bottom of my heart," I whispered, and Mrs. Stuart smiled. "No need, my dear. Healing is the gift I was given and that I am proud to share."

She rose and stood by the table.

I breathed deeply, looking around at what I supposed was the whole of the house. There was a narrow bed against the far wall. There were other wooden chairs that had the appearance of being handmade. There was a fire in the hearth, a clock, and a hanging lantern. I had never seen a house this small, so unencumbered with belongings, so filled with light.

But Eli lived there too. How could there be only one bed?

His grandmother's concentration was on the leaves. She was studying, choosing, transferring some into the large bowl. She held up a small green bunch. "Sorrel," she muttered. Another: "Yellow archangel." Another: "Coltsfoot, to reduce the swelling and inflammation."

She chose, rejected.

All of the ones selected went together onto a board.

I watched as she chose one, studied it, muttered something, and dropped it back in its own small bowl. "Lady's mantle," she said. "It stanches bleeding. I do not think we have need of that."

From a drawer below the table she produced a knife that resembled a small hatchet. It could have been a weapon.

With a speed I had never seen anyone use when handling a knife, she chopped all the leaves on the board and scooped them into the large bowl.

"Eli and I find my ingredients," she said cheerfully. "They all grow around here. You just have to look and know the properties of each. There are poisonous ones too. But not in my house."

"Yes. He knew which plant to use to ease my nettle sting," I said.

Her smile showed me a dimple. "I have used a dock leaf

on many of *his* stings. He was always roaming and exploring when he was a boy."

She took a wooden instrument shaped like an upside-down mushroom, added some drops of a clear liquid to the bowl, and began pounding.

Pound, pound, pound.

"There's foxglove and woody nightshade to be found by the roadside," she said. "Poisonous, malignant. The nightshade has bright purple or yellow flowers. Very pretty. Reminds us that something that looks enticing can be deadly."

"And what is this?" I asked, lifting a small bottle, filled with liquid that was white as milk.

"That is a sleeping potion," she said. "Made from reishi mushrooms and the oil of hops. I have used a drop or two myself when I have been too worried to sleep."

I somehow knew her worries would be for Eli.

We were both quiet as she filled another bowl with water that had been warmed and bathed my foot and ankle. The water turned from clear to the palest pink. Gently she dried the wound and went back to her pounding.

The leaves came together in a green paste that she lifted and sniffed.

Her smile at me was one of satisfaction. "It is ready."

I smiled too, but mine was a false smile. She was going

to put this strange mixture on my ankle, on the open sores? I had acquiesced. I'd been fascinated. But would this concoction really help? Or would it cause more harm? Could I, at this last moment, reject her ministrations? Could I —

She had turned from me and taken a long, narrow cloth from where it lay on one of the other chairs. "Now we will spread on the paste and bind it up."

I could do nothing.

I held up my foot. Using her fingers, she spread the compote over the wounds and wrapped the cloth tight around them, securing it in place. It was easy to see that she had tended to cuts many times before.

It was cool and soothing, and I could not resist a sigh of pleasure.

"There," she said. "You will need to return tomorrow so I can ascertain if it needs further attention. Now shall we have a cup of tea before you leave?"

She brought a teapot, black and battered, from the hob. "I hope you like it strong," she said.

"Yes, thank you," I responded, although in truth I did not.

I slid my stocking over the bandage and winced.

"It will ease," Mrs. Stuart said in a kindly tone. "I promise you that, my dear. You will be surprised how speedily it will feel better."

Tears sprang into my eyes. For the first time since I had arrived, I felt true goodness and kindness directed toward me.

"You may want to have your uncle Caleb look at it. You know he was an apothecary?"

I nodded. I would not want any such thing.

"Have you eaten?" she asked me. "I can give you a scone and blaeberry jam. I like to make jam from the berries I find. Do not worry. I do not use woody nightshade or foxglove." There was mischief in her eyes, and I knew this to be a joke, possibly to stir me from my nervousness, so I laughed.

We sat at the table and drank our tea, which was not only strong but bitter. The scone was good, though, and the blaeberry jam just sweet enough to be an antidote to the tea.

"Eli tells me you are to be two years at your uncle's house," Mrs. Stuart said.

"Yes. Till my eighteenth birthday." I found myself intensely curious about Eli, I was not sure why. Merely that he was the only other person I had talked to since I came, except for my uncle and aunt, of course, and Mrs. Kitteridge with the beringed fingers.

"Eli was kind to bring me," I said. "Does he live here with you?"

"He has an addition to my house that he built for himself. We have a common wall. I can knock on it if I want him. He concerns himself about me, though there is no need. I am perfectly capable and sufficient unto myself."

I nodded to say I agreed with her.

"Sometimes he has to go away for several weeks, but he always comes back." She paused. "More tea?"

"Thank you, but no," I told her.

"Another scone?"

"That would be delightful." I fissled my brains to think of a way to ask more questions about Eli. What was this consuming need I had to find out about him?

"Does he work in Brindle?"

"Oh, no!" She fetched a scone and set it in front of me. "He is involved in his own work."

"And what is that?" I pretended great interest in spreading the blaeberry jam on my scone.

There was a moment's silence and then she said, "You will need to ask him. He is a very private person."

Had I been too forthright? Had I been snubbed? No. When I looked at Mrs. Stuart, her expression was as pleasant and friendly as it had been before.

She asked me about my mother and father and sympathized. It was not false sympathy. I could tell. I remembered my uncle with his perfunctory "we offer our condolences." This was different.

"Eli's parents passed on also," she said. "That was why he came back to live with me for a longer time than is usual."

"Oh," I said. "He is an orphan too. Like me."

"Yes."

A painting of a woman and a man hung on the wall. She saw me looking at it.

"Those were Eli's parents," she said.

The man was dressed in dark velvet breeches and a white ruffled shirt with a blue velvet waistcoat cut in the new fashion. The woman wore an Empire-style dress with a low neckline. At her throat was a delicate chain embellished with a shining purple pendant. Her hair was a deep, dark red. The artist had caught the tenderness and charm of her expression.

"They are very handsome," I said.

She sighed. "Yes. That was the dress Miranda wore the night she drowned."

She added more honey to her tea and closed her eyes.

When she was through with what I assumed was a moment of private grief, she asked me about my long journey to get there and about Edinburgh, and I had an impression that she wanted to speak no more about Eli or his parents. Maybe she felt she had said too much. But that was ridiculous. She had actually said little.

I told her of the city's ornamental gardens and about the castle high on the hill.

"It is a beautiful city," I said. "I hope to return to it in two years' time."

We drank our tea.

A short time later, she said, "I will summon Eli now, if you are ready."

I rose from the chair. "I have troubled him enough," I said. "I no longer require his help. I know my way back."

Why had I made such a pronouncement? I knew I *did* want to trouble him again, to have him walk with me. I was asserting my independence and demonstrating that although I might have appeared curious about Eli, I had no interest in him. As I'd promised myself.

Foolish girl! My mother would have said I was spiting myself and I would be sorry for it. I was already sorry.

"I thank you again for your ministrations," I said. "I do believe that already the pain in my ankle has lessened."

"I'm glad to hear it. But it would be wise to have Eli walk with you, this one time. Your ankle may be weak. You might need his help."

She leaned across her narrow bed and knocked on the wall.

"It is not necessary——" I began.

"It may be."

"Very well."

I was going to have his company again. I had demurred politely, but I had been overruled. I could not keep the pleasure out of my voice, or, I imagined, out of my face. I was aware that the color was rising in my cheeks, and I took a deep breath. I must stay calm. What was the matter with me? I was acting and thinking like a silly goose.

Mrs. Stuart came across to me and took my hands in hers. "My dear. You have faced too many distressing events. I sympathize." She paused, and I saw her bite her lip. "But I do want to warn you. Do not give your heart to Eli. If you do, it will be broken."

I pulled my hands away. Was she deranged?

"Dear girl," she said softly. "You think me a meddlesome old woman. But I saw how you looked at him. You should know. Eli is forbidden."

CHAPTER SEVEN

I STARED AT MRS. STUART. What . . . ? How dare she speak to me like this? She saw how I looked at him! That was laughable! As if I would ever fancy her grandson! As if . . . And what did she mean, "forbidden"? Forbidden by whom? To do what? Forbidden by her?

And there he was, standing in the open doorway.

"May I offer my arm again?" he asked. "For your return to Raven's Roost?"

"It is kind of you," I said stiffly. "But it is unnecessary. I am perfectly capable of going alone." How was I looking at him? I lowered my eyes.

He gave that slight shrug that I was becoming acquainted with. "If you prefer."

His grandmother glanced from one of us to the other. "Do not forget to come back tomorrow," she advised me.

"I will see how it feels. Perhaps there will be no need for further treatment." I tried to keep the indignation I felt out of my voice. *Do not give your heart to Eli,* indeed! As if I would! This ill-dressed, ungentlemanly person! He had aided me, of course. He had saved me from Lamb. But still . . .

"You must do what you think is best," his grandmother said.

"I will," I said. "And I thank you again." I bobbed my head, then hobbled past Eli, through the door and down the shell-lined path.

The sky did not seem as blue, the breeze not so sweet as I walked back. Perhaps there was about to be another change in the weather. Or perhaps I was in a different frame of mind. I told myself that I should be grateful. My ankle had required attention, and she had been more than kind. But I could not seem to lose my vexation. The thought that I might have been walking with Eli and not alone taunted me more than once. I chose to dismiss it.

Raven's Roost had the look of emptiness. No smoke rose from the chimney. There was no one about. Lamb would be inside, left to watch the house . . . and me.

I was seized with a sudden restlessness. I could go down again and sit on the rock where I had sat earlier. I would try not to think of Eli Stuart. Eli Stuart, who was forbidden. Like Adam and Eve, who had eaten of the forbidden fruit. Had it been worth it for them, or had the price they'd paid been too costly?

I looked across the ocean at the Sisters. My aunt and uncle were out there till the tide changed. When would that be? My knowledge of tides was rudimentary, but I thought that the tide came in, went out, came in again, went out again in a day and night cycle. That meant they would not be back till afternoon.

I gazed around me. If it were not for the weakness in my ankle, I would walk the mile to Brindle and see what was there. I would buy stockings to replace the ones I now wore that were almost tattered. My first glimpse of the town had been unpleasant. But if I was to be there for a long while, I needed to take stock of it again.

Then I remembered the horse. I would ride him! The idea excited me and lifted my spirits.

I limped to the animal enclosure. The horse was

small and old. He stood patiently and lifted his head to inspect me.

I spoke to him gently and ventured close to stroke his nose. "Shall we go for a ride?" I whispered.

I saw no saddle or bridle. They would no doubt be in the shed, which was locked. I tried the door, pushing on it, angry now and frustrated. It was immovable. I walked around it. In back I saw two old carriage wheels, a table missing a leg, a rain barrel half full of water. No saddle. No bridle.

So, I would walk despite the pain. I was not, not, going to be trapped there.

Lamb watched me impassively as I went into the house.

"Good dog," I whispered. "Nice Lamb."

He moved to the bottom of the stair as I went up to my room. The door to my aunt and uncle's room was closed. Should I look inside?

Curiosity killed the cat, I knew. But I would take my chances. I reached for the doorknob and immediately, from the bottom of the stairs, came a low, frightening growl.

Lamb was standing now, his paws on the lowest step. I quickly took my hand from the knob, and he lay down again. But the golden hairs along his back were still raised. Had he been told to keep me out of their room? I couldn't believe it. I knew some animals could be trained to do tricks, but this was different. He chilled my blood.

I retrieved my purse from the drawer. There were three sovereigns in it and ten shillings. The sovereigns I left where they were. I wrapped two of the silver shillings in a handkerchief and put them in the pocket of my dress. In the other pocket was the sharpened quill. I let it be.

I put my weight on my foot and groaned with pain. "Dangnabit!" I fumed. There was no chance that I could walk a mile on it. I was there, and there I must stay.

I got my book of poetry from the dresser, went back to the living room, and settled at the table. But even Lord Byron could not keep my attention.

I studied Lamb. Would he allow me to explore Raven's Roost if I kept away from their room?

There was not much to the house.

My aunt Minnie kept a clean and tidy home. The grate had been shined, the mantel dusted, the floor scrubbed. The table where we'd eaten gleamed, as did the heavy silver candlestick in its center. The violin was propped against the far wall. There was a door at the back of the kitchen.

Lamb did not move as I opened it and peered in.

There were heavy waterproof boots, waterproof coats, two oars, a rolled-up canvas that might have been a small sail. A saddle—not a sidesaddle, bridle, and reins hung on a peg.

Praise be!

With difficulty, I dragged the saddle outside and went back for the bridle and reins.

Lamb paid no heed.

The horse stood quietly as I put the saddle and bridle on him and fixed the reins.

"What is your name?" I whispered to him. "Do you have a name?"

In this strange place, I would not have been startled if he'd answered. I shook my head. Such nonsensical thinking would only deter me from my mission.

"I will call you Dobbin," I said. "Is that all right?"

With difficulty, I got my uninjured foot into the stirrup and was on.

"Go, Dobbin!" I whispered.

He walked slowly through the wooden gateposts. I knew I should push the gate closed again, but I was in a hurry to be gone. "Stay!" I told the hens that were huddled under a lean-to shelter. If they wandered and became lost, I suspected I would be in great trouble. For that, and for taking the horse without permission.

The horse and I ambled along the road I'd come on

last night. There was no way to hasten him, but it did not matter. My aunt and uncle would not be back till the tide turned, and that would be much later.

I was accustomed to riding sidesaddle. But I was quite comfortable. What a pretty sight I must look, I thought, with my dress raised, my pantaloons exposed on either side of Dobbin's back, my bedraggled stockings, no bonnet on my head to save my skin and to tame my curls, no gloves to cover my hands. Not correct attire for a young lady. How Eli Stuart would smile at my concern with modesty! Thanks be that he couldn't see me.

I could still hear the sea, and my lips tasted of salt.

When I twisted around in the saddle and looked back, I could see Raven's Roost and several other houses jumbled along Brindle Point. I could see the house among the trees where Eli lived.

My mind suddenly filled with him. His blue-green eyes, his smile, which I had seen only twice but remembered with such vividness, it made me gasp. What ailed me? Why was I so beset with thoughts of him?

Which house was Daphne's? Daphne who pined for him? Was she beautiful?

"Go, Dobbin," I said. "Go quickly so I have no time to think or wonder. Carry me to Brindle."

CHAPTER EIGHT

I SAW THE VILLAGE IN THE distance, and as we got closer, I realized there was no noisy disturbance, no groups of jeering onlookers to taunt me. It appeared to be a normal town, with men and women, suitably attired, in the streets. There was a cart filled with peat, probably taken from a nearby bog, and two horses tied to a railing.

Then I became aware of the faces peering out at me from behind curtains. House after house had curtains closed, twitching to indicate watchers behind them. A shiver crawled along my body. I noticed that those we met stared at me with more than curiosity. There was hostility. And the smiles I offered were not returned.

We passed a blacksmith's shop, where the smell of burning hooves wafted toward us. The blacksmith stopped hammering and came to stand at the door as we passed. I was sure I was a strange sight, though he called out, "Good mornin', Mistress," before he took off his cap and scratched his head and called again, "Mistress! What is your business here?"

I did not answer.

Here was a produce shop with a barrel of cabbages on display outside.

Here a tavern with a swinging board proclaiming, THE FISHERMAN'S INN.

Next to it was a fancy-looking establishment called Jackdaws. I led Dobbin over and managed to slide down from his back. A man stopped to watch.

I looped the reins around the railing.

"Good morn," he said, doffing his hat. "I am Clifton MacIntyre, mayor of Brindle." His eyes were small, and a drooping mustache hid his mouth.

I tried to smooth my hair. "I am happy to meet you, sir."

"You may not think Brindle sufficiently important to have a mayor," he said in a voice both pompous and patronizing. "But we are quite a thriving community, though small. We get visitors from towns afar. They come to shop at Jackdaws." He nodded slightly toward the fancy shop behind him.

"I am sure," I said.

"And you, Mistress, are?"

"I am Josie Ferguson, niece to Caleb Ferguson of Brindle Point." At my words, I saw his face change. Change to what? I wasn't certain. He was less watchful now, as if reassured. That I did know.

"You are here to stay?"

"For a long time," I told him. "But not forever."

He absently leaned over and stroked Dobbin's head. "I should have been more observant," he said. "You are riding your uncle's horse."

"Yes." I smoothed Dobbin's mane. When I got back to Raven's Roost, I would find a comb and untangle it.

"Well," the mayor said at last. "Your aunt and uncle are fine people. Please give them my regards."

"I shall," I informed him, though indeed I was hoping to be back at Raven's Roost before they missed me. I watched him walk away, then curiosity tempted me and I pushed open the door of Jackdaws. Perhaps I would find stockings. A polite bell tinkled. Sun slanted through the windows, illuminating the interior, and I caught my breath. I felt as if I'd stepped into another world, a hushed hidden world.

Aladdin's cave.

Around me and displayed on polished tables and shelves was bric-a-brac of all kinds. China angels, china dogs, snuffboxes, jewelry, ladies' fans, some of which were broken and stained. A glimmering blue dress was spread across a chest. And there were stockings, finer and less serviceable than any I'd ever worn. Those would not do for me. I saw a ship's steering wheel made of gleaming mahogany. There was a prie-dieu, all faded scarlet and gold. I had the uncomfortable feeling that someone was watching me, but when I turned around, I saw that it was a ship's figurehead, a beautiful plaster woman with golden locks and a bare bosom. For a moment, I imagined her on the prow of some great ship, facing the wind, reaching out for unknown territory. What had happened to that ship? How had the figurehead come here?

A piano stood next to me and, without thinking, I tapped on the keys. Sound shivered out, and I lifted my fingers as if they'd been burned.

A woman, very stylish in a dove gray dress and shoes with buckles, came out from a curtain at the rear. Her yellow hair was parted in the middle with small kiss curls clamped around her face. I wondered why she had not appeared before. I could have easily stolen something. But then I became aware of all the mirrors that hung on the walls. She would have watched me as I strayed around the shop.

She greeted me with a smile. "Good morning to you, Mistress. Thank you for looking in on my humble place of business. I am the proprietress, Mrs. Esmeralda Davies. But please call me by my given name. In Brindle we are all family. Have you traveled far to visit Jackdaws?"

"Not at all," I said. "Today I came from Raven's Roost. I am niece to Caleb and Minnie Ferguson. I am here to stay with them on Brindle Point."

"Ah." It was a long-drawn-out exclamation. "Your aunt and uncle come in here often."

"Indeed?" I thought of Raven's Roost and its plain interior. The only extravagances that I had seen were the grand table, the dresser in my room, the serviette ring, the splendid three-armed candlestick, and the violin. I could have been mistaken when I thought they'd retrieved them from their old home. Perhaps they had bought them here.

"Are you interested in something I might provide?" Mistress Davies asked. "A dress? You would look very pretty in that blue shantung."

"Thank you. But I have no use for a dress."

She glanced up at me. "I have a lot of merchandise. May

I suggest something else? Forgive me, but I can see that you are in need of stockings and shoes."

"My foot is injured." I tried to raise it above the hem of my dress. "My shoe is tight on it."

She nodded. Even the movement of her head did not stir the circle of kiss curls on her forehead. "I have slippers . . . dancing slippers. A little fancy perhaps, but soft and comfortable for time at home. They might be of help to you till your ankle heals."

She disappeared behind the curtain and reappeared holding a pair of blue satin slippers, beaded on top. "They belong with the dress, but I am willing to let them go their separate ways."

I took them from her. I had never seen anything so delicate, so exquisite. They were inappropriate, ridiculous even, but I wanted them. As I held them, the picture came, unbidden, of me, in these blue jeweled slippers and my white muslin dress, dancing with Eli Stuart. We were waltzing, my head on his shoulder, his lips against my hair . . .

"Do you wish to purchase the slippers?" Esmeralda asked, rather sharply. "One shilling."

I felt dizzy, as though I had indeed been dancing. "Please," I said, and took one of the coins from my pocket.

"You are certain you do not want the dress?" she

asked in a coaxing tone. "They go well together." She lifted the edge of the gleaming skirt and let it fall. But not before I had seen, printed across the wooden chest, the name BONIFACE.

I stared. That was the name on my aunt's serviette ring. Had she sold some of her family possessions here?

I looked around. On a crate were laid out three pairs of men's trousers of various lengths. Should I? I recalled my aunt Minnie's apparel and, at the same time, thought of the look of me on Dobbin's back. If my aunt and uncle should allow me to ride Dobbin while I was there, a dress would be unsuitable. I could, if I desired, wear trousers under the dress. Strange and unladylike, but better than displaying my pantaloons and perhaps my garters. My aunt and uncle would see them and know I'd gone to Brindle. But no matter.

One pair of trousers seemed to be altogether smaller than the others, perhaps sewn for a boy rather than a man.

"How much for these?" I asked Esmeralda.

She tittered, picked up a fan to cover her mouth, and said, "A shilling will be plenty. Do you plan on emulating your aunt Minnie?"

"Perhaps." I took the second shilling from my pocket and gave it to her. Mrs. Chandler — worse, my mother — would faint if she saw what I was purchasing.

"The trousers will be useful for the work," Esmeralda said, all saleswoman again.

The polite doorbell announced another visitor to Jackdaws.

"My word! We keep meeting," Mrs. Kitteridge said to me on entering the shop. Her beringed fingers shot off sparks.

"You have met Mistress Ferguson?" the proprietor asked, her quick glance stabbing toward each of us in turn.

"Please call me Josie," I said, and added jestingly, "I hear tell we are all family in Brindle."

"Indeed." Mrs. Kitteridge inclined her head. "I was introduced to Josie this morn. By Eli Stuart," she told Esmeralda.

"Eli Stuart!" All of the proprietress's smiles and greetings disappeared. "Do not speak his name in my establishment!" She glowered at me. "Does your uncle know you have been in his company?"

"No," I answered. "I do not see why he would object."

"You do not see?" she snorted. "Eli Stuart should be driven out of this town. He does not belong here."

Mrs. Kitteridge interrupted. "You know full well, Esmeralda, that we have done our best to be rid of him. Three times. And three times we failed. None want to try again. They do not dare. The Decree of Three . . . It is accepted he may not be killed."

"Sometimes I despair of the absurdities of the people around me." Esmeralda sniffed to show her disgust. "The Decree of Three applies to animals. Not people. It is to save the livestock."

"It is to show they are under divine protection," Mrs. Kitteridge said, clasping her hands in a gesture of supplication.

Esmeralda's voice was cold. "It is superstitious nonsense. If I had the means to do it, I'd take care of Eli Stuart myself."

She would get rid of Eli Stuart? He could not be killed?

Esmeralda turned her hard stare on me. "I advise that you keep your distance from him, Mistress Josie, lest you too come into disfavor."

"Shush, Esmeralda!" Mrs. Kitteridge soothed. "You are frightening the lass!" Her voice turned brisk. "Now. I have come with something in mind. Since my Daphne saw the blue shantung dress, she is convinced she must have it. You know I can never deny that girl anything she desires."

"Even Eli Stuart? Even though you know how he abhors us?" Esmeralda's voice was almost a hiss.

Mrs. Kitteridge went on as if there had been no dispute,

though I noticed how she fumbled with her words. "He does not abhor Daphne. I have already told her she cannot have the dress. It is altogether too dear. But it is her seventeenth birthday, so I have relented and come to town without her. I will purchase it as a surprise."

"You will need to shorten it," Esmeralda said with a sly smirk.

Mrs. Kitteridge waved her beringed hand dismissively. "I can do that." She addressed me. "Josie! You must come and call on her. She loves to have company." She seemed to suddenly become aware of the trousers I had hung across my arm and the blue satin slippers I still held. "Oh, those are the matching slippers. I must buy those also."

I childishly put the slippers behind my back. "I am afraid I have already purchased them."

Esmeralda, excellent proprietress that she was and sensing a second sale, said quickly, "She is correct, Mrs. Kitteridge. But I have another pair of exquisite slippers from the same source. The latest fashion. They are silver and are perhaps even prettier than the blue ones."

She disappeared behind the beaded curtain and came back with the silver slippers.

Mrs. Kitteridge's pout vanished. "Oh, yes. These are lovely. I will have them." She turned them over appreciatively and asked, "From the same source?"

"Indeed."

"Everything from there has been high-class," Mrs. Kitteridge said. "I wonder if this next one . . . ?"

Esmeralda gave her a telling glance, though I did not know just what she was telling.

Mrs. Kitteridge clapped her hand to her mouth, and her rings dazzled, red and blue and scarlet. "Sometimes I forget," she said. "We are not yet all family."

"Thank you for coming into Jackdaws, Josie," Esmeralda purred. "You must hurry home. A prodigious storm is on the way. Angus MacCormick came by to . . . to warn me."

"Is it certain?" Mrs. Kitteridge raised her eyebrows and smiled broadly. "The Lord be thanked!"

I wondered. Was everyone in Brindle so pious? And so secretive?

"It does not look like a storm is approaching," I said.

"Oh, yes. It will come this very night. Angus Mac-Cormick has the weather sense. He is never wrong."

"Did Angus MacCormick tell them of the distance . . . ? Are the men readying?" Mrs. Kitteridge asked.

I looked from one of them to the other. Did they enjoy storms? The men were readying for it. Boarding windows, perhaps, or checking roofs.

Esmeralda closed her eyes as if in despair. "Be quiet, Mrs. Kitteridge. You are altogether too talkative!" She gave me a turgid smile. "This small talk is meaningless and discourteous to you. I apologize for our rudeness. But you'd best be off, Mistress Josie. Remember me to your aunt and uncle." She turned her shoulder on me.

I had been dismissed.

CHAPTER NINE

I HAD SEEN LITTLE MORE OF BRINDLE than the
main street and Jackdaws, but there was no time now.

I urged Dobbin to move a little faster as we made our
journey back to Raven's Roost. The morning had passed,
Angus MacCormick had said a storm was coming, and he
was never wrong. We were already into the afternoon.
I was becoming more and more concerned that my aunt
and uncle would have returned. And that the storm might
come early.

"Go, Dobbin," I told him, but he did not alter his gait.

As I bumped up and down on the narrow road, I tried to sort through what I had heard and seen in Brindle. How could a small town, perhaps even a village, have a shop such as Jackdaws? What of the shantung dress and other articles that were all "from the same source"? I had an uneasy feeling that I could not define. Mrs. Kitteridge had said too much, and I was "not yet family." They need not be concerned. I had understood little of their conversation. There had been an air of secrecy about the two of them and about the town, an undertow of menace. And what about Eli Stuart? They wanted nothing but to be rid of him and could not manage it.

The Decree of Three. What was that?

The sun that had been shining was shining no longer. Dark clouds had gathered and hung heavy with rain.

I pushed my blue slippers deeper into my pocket to keep them dry. The trousers, I knew, would wash themselves in the rain.

The wind was gusting now, lifting the skirt of my frock, taking my breath from me. "Come on, Dobbin," I urged. "Faster!"

Lamb obeyed my aunt Minnie, but Dobbin did not care what I wanted. We proceeded at our funereal pace.

The rain had started, pelting down in a slant that soon soaked me and the trousers I'd draped over the horse's neck. I was almost glad to see the roof of Raven's Roost, although I was not overjoyed to think of being inside again with Lamb for my only companion.

But when I reached the house, I found that I was not to be alone. My uncle Caleb came roaring out of the door.

"Where were you girl? Where did you go? Sleekiting around again, were you, sticking your nose into my business?" He was dressed in a warm coat and boots, and his hideous ears were hidden by a black knit cap, like a tea cozy.

"And taking Nag," he spat.

I tried to give him stare for stare.

"Get down!" he ordered. "Get down and get in the house."

I was aware of my wet dress clinging to me, exposing my undergarments again as I got both legs to the one side and slid off Dobbin's back.

My uncle was glaring at my ankle. His eyes narrowed.

"What is that wrapping on your foot?"

"I met a woman who attended to my wound," I said belligerently. Water dripped from me in a steady stream. I gathered my hair and wrung it out. "It was infected by Lamb's bite. She applied a potion."

My heart was beating too fast. He was in a rage.

"What woman? There is only one on Brindle Point who believes herself a healer."

All my instincts urged me to be careful. "Mrs. Stuart. She was very kind."

"Come ye inside, Caleb," Aunt Minnie shouted. "You'll get your death of cold."

She stood in the doorway, one hand on Lamb's head.

My uncle paid her no mind.

I was not prepared for the shout of anger that exploded from him.

"Mrs. Stuart, was it?" He grabbed my arm. "You stay away from her. And from her weasel of a grandson." His face was so close to mine that his spittle sprayed across my face, and I could tell he was going to strike me.

I took a step back.

Lamb growled.

"Easy, Lamb!" my aunt called out. "Easy, Caleb. Remember what we spoke about? Time will pass."

It wasn't hard to realize that they had no more desire to have me than I had to stay. But there was the monthly payment. And the promise of the hundred guineas. My stomach was snarled. I looked at my uncle, the terrible red of his face, the spittle on his lips, his harsh words. How was I to stay for two long years?

At my aunt's shout, he let loose of my arm.

"I remember, woman," he said. "But I will not hold my

tongue. You are not to go near either one of them again, you hear?" he ordered me. "I forbid it."

Even in the tension of the moment, the word *forbid* resonated in my mind. "He is forbidden." Forbidden by my aunt and uncle?

I slid my hand into my pocket and clutched the blue slippers. "Uncle Caleb," I said, fighting the irrational shake in my voice, "I appreciate that you and Aunt Minnie are sheltering me. But I do not take kindly to intimidation. It was not my father's wish that you should rule over me when he arranged for me to be here and provided money for my keep. I do not expect you to be always affectionate toward me. However, I do not care for being ordered. We will live in better harmony if we treat one another with consideration."

My uncle scowled. "Do not be impudent. You will come inside and put that saddle and bridle back where you found them."

"You were in Jackdaws," Aunt Minnie said. It was not a question but a statement. She nodded toward the trousers.

"Yes," I said, and nothing more.

Dobbin stood, patiently waiting. I petted his nose, then led him again into the enclosure. The five hens were still there.

Though I was forced to hobble, neither my aunt nor my uncle helped me as I dragged the saddle and bridle and reins back to where they had been, even though I had to make two excursions into and out of the house. The only one who watched me was Lamb.

I had never been so wet or so cold. Shivers chased along my legs.

They were in the sitting room, which I had to pass through again to get to the stair. Aunt Minnie was at the table polishing the silver candlestick with a cloth dipped in white powder. She didn't look up as she addressed me. "Did you make the acquaintance of the grandson while you were being attended to by Doss Stuart?"

"No," I said. I had made the grandson's acquaintance earlier, but I was not going to reveal that.

"Stay away from them," she said.

"Why?"

"Because we say so. While you are in our house, you will do as you're bid. Put those trousers by the fire to dry. There is porridge on the hob. Spoon yourself a bowlful and take it with you to your room. I will call you later."

The trousers began to steam as the heat of the fire reached them.

Neither of them spoke as I fetched a bowl, filled it, and

limped to the stair. My aunt handed me a lit candle in a tarnished holder.

"Josie?"

"Yes, Auntie?"

She turned from the table while I stood waiting for what was to come next. "Stay here."

She opened the door to the storage room, disappeared, and came back with a dark garment, which she handed to me.

I shook it out. It was a thick jersey with a name in red stamped on the chest. SEA URCHIN.

"It is oiled wool. If you are to work with us, you will need this to go along with the trousers."

It will be easier if I accede to what they want, I thought. *Time will pass. I need to remember that too.*

"When will I go fishing with you?" I asked. "I know nothing about it, but I am willing to learn and to help."

My uncle gave a short laugh.

My aunt's eyes seemed to bore into me. "Not yet," she said. "But soon."

I felt that gaze on my back as I went up the stairs.

My dress was soaked, and so were my undergarments. I took them off and put on my nightdress, then tried on the jersey. It was immense, coming down to my knees. The sleeves hung over my hands. I rolled them up and already felt the warmth. Some sailor or fisherman had worn this before me.

I sat on the flowered quilt and took the slippers from the pocket of my dress, which lay in a clump on the floor. The blue silk of them was damp but not stained. I was inordinately relieved.

I slid my good foot into one of them. The candlelight shone on the beads so they twinkled when I moved. It fitted perfectly, like Cinderella's slipper. Where was the prince? I did not like the image that sprang into my mind at the thought of the prince, so I shook my head and carried the slippers across to where my white muslin dress hung and set them beneath it.

I undid the bandage and examined my foot and ankle. It was not difficult to see that the wounds were already healing, thanks to Mrs. Stuart.

I sat then in my nightdress with the SEA URCHIN jersey on top and ate every drop of the porridge. It was still hot and deliciously salty. My fingers crept up under the wool jersey and found the opal pin at the neck of my nightgown. When my mother had given me this, she had expected that I would have a comfortable, happy life. "My beautiful girl," she had called me.

I did not believe myself beautiful, though I was aware

that my looks must be pleasing. It was not a knowledge I dwelled on. Since I was fourteen, boys and young men had clustered about me, being attentive, paying me awkward compliments. I was never sure I completely believed them.

"Your hair curls so becomingly! It is golden brown, the color of a new penny!" "I cannot describe the way I feel when I am with you. You are by far the most exquisite girl of my acquaintance!"

Their admiration embarrassed me, and sometimes, unfortunately, I would laugh at the wrong moment. Then I felt unkind, though I understood that my laughter came to cover my discomfort.

Did Eli Stuart think my appearance agreeable? Would I laugh if he told me so? I shook my head. What nonsense thoughts came into my head!

I discarded the jersey and crawled under the flowered quilt, my thoughts so muddled and on edge that I thought I would never sleep. But I did.

When I woke, it was completely dark. Rain slashed against the window, dropping noisily into the basin I'd emptied earlier. I could hear the thud of the surf on the beach and the rattle of the tree limbs outside my window.

I'd been told to wait for my aunt to call me, but I would not tarry.

I dressed again in dry clothes and went downstairs.

The fire had been restoked with turf, and it blazed and sparked in the hearth. An iron griddle was pushed to the side of the flames. My trousers gave off a not-unpleasant smell of drying cloth.

Lamb lifted his head to gaze at me, then slept again.

It was a homey scene and should have reassured me, but it did not.

My uncle sat on the wooden settle with the Bible in his hand. My aunt was mixing something in a brown bowl. She glanced at me. "I did not call."

"No," I said. "The rain is already filling up the basin."

She worked the mixture into a ball with her hands, patted it down, and carried it to the griddle. I saw that it was to be a bannock.

My uncle's lips moved as he read from the book.

I started again. "I was unable to sleep the first night. Shall I . . . ?

"Go outside. Get the bucket. Put it in place," my aunt said, picking up bellows and blowing the turf embers so they flared. Yellow and orange smoke rose, then subsided.

"If the bucket fills, empty it and put it back. Sleep or not, whatever suits you."

I wished I knew some curse words, but I did not. Behind her back, I childishly stuck out my tongue, then went outside as I was, without cloak or shawl.

The wind almost knocked me over. I staggered to where I remembered the pump to be, but there was no bucket beside it. Then I heard it trundling somewhere close where it had blown over and found it, guided only by the sound. How cozy the house looked with smoke curling wind-crooked from the chimney, the sitting room window pale and shining with candlelight. The appearance lied.

I turned from it and stood for a moment, staring down at the sea.

Monstrous black rollers rumbled in to smash on the sand and shingle. I saw the whites of them as they broke. Sand blew, stinging my face. I rubbed the rain from my eyes. Someone was walking on the beach close to the surf in the dark of the storm. I could not distinguish if it was man or woman, but there was an uneasy prickling at the back of my neck.

I hurried back to the house.

My uncle was reaching up to the small cupboard as I entered. I saw him lock it and drop what I took to be the key into the Toby Jug that sat close by it. He heard me at the door and swung around. "Dinner and prayers will be early tonight," he said. "Your aunt and I have business. There will be men coming, men who are our . . ."

He seemed unable to find the word.

"Our associates." Aunt Minnie supplied the word. She had her back to us as she turned the bannock on the griddle.

"Our associates will come," he went on. "We will be busy with the fishing. You will remain in your room."

Perhaps he did not know of the curiosity that was built into my character. Perhaps he did not remember that I had told him how I disliked being ordered.

"Is it not a bad night for the fishing?" I asked. "The sea is raging."

My uncle suddenly grabbed my arm. "If you are to live with us, you will have to learn not to ask questions," he growled.

"I apologize." But I suddenly knew. They were not going fishing. They and their associates had other plans, and those plans were connected with the conversation between Esmeralda and Mrs. Kitteridge. Something was happening, something illicit, and I needed to know what it was. They would leave Lamb to guard me. Somehow I would deal with Lamb.

CHAPTER TEN

THE CANDLE FLAME flickered shadows on the walls, touched the white dress, lighted the sparkles on the blue dancing slippers that waited beneath it.

I stood on the bed and peered through the window. Rain poured down it in a steady stream, and I could see nothing through the fog of it. I ran my fingers along its edges. It had been opened in the past. The cords to raise and lower the sash were still there, but time and weather had stuck it closed. I took the quill from my pocket and poked its point into its lowest edge. A crumb of rotten wood fell onto my bed.

I caught my breath, then prodded some more.

I could do it. If I could get this unstuck, and if I could get the window to push up, I had a way out. I jabbed harder. The spike of the quill snapped off and stuck in the rotted wood.

No! No! No!

"Josie!" That was my aunt calling from the bottom of the stairs.

I looked despairingly at the embedded quill point but comforted myself that I could not, in any case, have moved the window in time for tonight.

The sitting room and kitchen were warm and filled with the smells of fresh bannock. The table was set with plates and a jug of milk and the big pat of yellow butter.

"Sit you down," my uncle said, addressing me but not looking at me. My aunt immediately came from the stove to join us.

My uncle stood to give the blessing, but there was an air of excitement and urgency in his voice. He spoke so quickly, the words ran together.

"Some hae meat an' canna eat . . ."

The plate my aunt set before me had two coddled eggs

on it. She sliced the bannock and shoved it across the table toward me. It was still warm.

I spread butter on it. "This is so tasty," I said. "You are an excellent cook, Auntie." I acknowledged to myself that I said the words not only because they were true but also to gain her favor.

She grunted.

By the hearth, Lamb wolfed down what I took to be the remains of the fish stew we had partaken of last night.

"Eat up," my uncle said to me. "There is no time for talk."

Perhaps, I thought, *there will be no time for readings or prayers tonight either.* But I was wrong.

"Stay where you are," he told me when we'd finished eating. My aunt leaned across the table and lit the three red candles. My uncle opened the big Bible and read aloud. I tried to keep my mind on the words, but that was beyond my capabilities.

"Josie!"

I realized that the reading had ended, and I rose from my chair and knelt for the prayer.

Their eyes were closed. I reached behind me, slid the knife I'd used from the table and slipped it beneath my skirt. A knife to pry open the window!

Aunt Minnie's hard brandy-ball eyes were open now and fixed on me.

"Put it back," she whispered.

Denial would have been to no avail. She had seen.

"Be quiet," Uncle Caleb said loudly. "I am speaking with the Lord."

I wriggled the knife from where I had hidden it and eased it back in place.

After a few more minutes, while my uncle conversed with God, I let my thoughts wander to the window upstairs. So how else . . .

My uncle suddenly called out, his voice loud enough to startle me from my musings.

"Minnie!"

My aunt stood and began to sing. I think it was a chant, the kind that I had heard were done in Papist churches, though not in our staid Presbyterian meeting halls.

"Lighten our darkness, we beseech Thee, O Lord . . ."

My uncle's eyes were closed, his chin quivered with emotion, his fingers caressed the growths on his ears.

My aunt's voice was strong and harsh but incredibly moving, as were the words.

"And by Thy great mercy defend us from all perils and dangers of this night."

There was a softness in my aunt's face as she sang.

The severe lines had smoothed out. She looked pure in heart.

Warmth suffused me. Perhaps I was mistaken in suspecting them of nefarious doings? Perhaps tonight *was* just a business meeting to discuss the price of fish or the best fishing grounds.

My aunt sat and bowed her head, and my uncle spoke.

"Josie! Get up to your room and stay there. Do not come out until we summon you."

I stared at him. My devout uncle had vanished. This change of tone, of attitude, jarred me back to my earlier instincts. This was not to be an ordinary meeting.

I went across to the hearth and retrieved the trousers.

They were dry and warm from the fire. I hung them over my arm, took the bucket and my candle, and started upstairs. Once I turned on the stairs and saw my aunt bend to Lamb and knew she was whispering to him. They both glanced up at me.

Instantly I knew.

As I had suspected, Lamb was to guard me tonight. He had been given his orders. I was not to be allowed out of the house.

Outside the storm blustered, thumping the tree branches as if some demon was trying to get in. The sea smashed on the shore far below.

I heard a sliding sound outside my door, the sounds of a body settling.

Lamb was there, keeping me under close watch.

It was not long till I heard the whinnying of a horse somewhere outside. Then the sound of hoofbeats and the rattle of cart wheels. Voices.

I strained to hear, but the rumble of the storm kept the words from me.

Another horse and cart were arriving below. The associates were gathering.

There was laughter, a shout of "a good night for it," and the answering shout of "aye."

"It'll be here this hour. Angus MacCormick sent the word. It be's coming now. It's past Seal Cove, headed in the right direction. All it needs is a bit of help."

There was a guffaw of laughter.

I climbed again on my bed and tried to see outside, but there was only rain and mist.

More horses. Had I counted four?

I nibbled at my thumb.

But now there was a change. The voices were inside, down in the living room. I pressed my ear against the door. Only a muddle of sound and laughter.

What if Lamb knew me well enough now to let me out?

If I could just be on the stairs, I would be able to hear and then, by the conversations, to determine what was happening.

I took off my nightdress and attired myself in jersey and trousers, my last thick stockings, my shoes. The trousers fitted well enough. I had no mirror in which to see myself, but I could imagine the ugly cut of me.

I took a deep breath and eased the door open, just a finger's breadth.

A babble of noise came at me from below.

Lamb's head lifted, but he made no other move.

My hand on the doorknob was clammy as fish skin.

"Lamb," I whispered, and took a step out onto the landing.

He was up before I could say more. Every hair bristled. His lips were curled back on his teeth as he snarled.

I smashed the door shut.

Oh, my heaven! One more second, and he would have sprung at me.

I leaned against the inside wall, pressing my hand against the jolting of my heart.

I was imprisoned, and Lamb was my jailer.

But he hadn't attacked me when I had simply opened

the door and stayed inside my room. Could it be . . . ? Was I now trying to think like a dog?

It took every ounce of courage that I had to open the door again, just a pinch.

Through the narrow gap, I could see him, half asleep again, his giant head between his giant paws.

"Lamb?"

No movement from the dog.

The smell of strong spirits wafted up to me, making me want to sneeze. A sneeze could be disastrous. The need passed.

A few of the voices below were audible to me now. Some words jumbled over themselves; some were indistinguishable.

A man was speaking, gruff and loud. "We made a covenant, Caleb. Just us."

"Aye." Several voices. "We put a luck penny on it."

"You and Minnie agreed to it."

Lamb twitched and scratched his underbelly. I retreated a step and waited till he settled.

"Boris is right, Caleb. The fewer that's sharin', the better. You said it would be so —"

"But that was afore she came. She's to be here for two years." My uncle's strident voice.

I clenched my fists. I was the "she" they were arguing over.

My aunt Minnie, the only female voice in the room, shouted, "She'll be in agreement. I'll see to it. Caleb and I can use help . . . Who better than our own flesh and blood?"

"Does she have the boldness for it?" A high, piercing tone.

"We'll . . . she does. She'll . . . on it right soon, anyway."

Not every word was clear.

"Better with us than agin' us," somebody said.

In my mind's vision, I saw my uncle standing before them. How many were there? Four men, one woman? I imagined him scowling, fingering his ear, playing on the bumps like on an accordion, along one way, back the next. "'Twill not be this night," he went on, speaking so clearly that I could distinguish every word. "We first needed your take on it, and she needs trainin'. All right, men! Who is for us? Can we get a vote?"

There was mumbling below.

How I wished that I could rush down the stairs and scream at them, "I don't know what you are devising. But I wager it's villainous. It matters not how you vote. I will not be part of it."

I was shaking and bone-chilled.

There were shouts of "Aye." "Aye." "Aye."

"It's done, then. We'll get the lass ready for the next time. Minnie has her ways."

"Are we takin' Nag this night, Caleb?"

"Aye. An' you're the one to lead him, Bruce. Up and down, man. Up and down. Make sure you bind it tight."

There was some subdued laughter. "Aye. A light's no use to us if it falls off, Bruce. Ye remember the last time! Use a fisherman's knot."

My aunt Minnie yelled, "A brandy, then, to seal the pact afore the launching. The night's a-wastin'. There's four of us here'll be on the water. With luck, we'll need more than one trip."

"Aye. God please there'll be two or even three."

They were going to launch their boats. What else could it be? They weren't set on fishing. That I knew.

I gently closed the door, careful that Lamb did not hear me, and lay on my bed, imagining them riding tonight, dark and deadly on a dark and deadly sea.

CHAPTER ELEVEN

I LAY, MY BRAIN IN TURMOIL, the candle sputtering on the dresser. Two nights I'd spent in this bed, two uneasy nights.

All was quiet inside Raven's Roost. But outside, below my window, horses moved restlessly, whinnied, stomped their hooves.

Plop, plop, plop.

The monotonous sound of the rain falling into the bucket unstrung me.

It was not long till I heard voices below my window

and the new sounds of horses' hooves and the rattle of cart wheels. They were leaving? No. They were going to the boats. But why take the horses and the carts? The distance was no more than a stone's throw.

I replayed in my mind the overheard conversations. Some of their words had been about me. Some about Dobbin, whom they called Nag, and some about fisherman's knots and launching the boats.

Storm wind roared around the walls. A branch of the tree by my window banged the glass. *Let me in! Let me in!*

Smash harder, I thought. *Smash the glass into smithereens so I can climb through you and escape.*

I sat up. I would smash it. There was no time to be weak.

I hefted the candlestick. One blow to the glass, two.

Nervousness, fear, excitement choked me.

The window cracked, then fell out with a splintery crash.

Rain and freezing air rushed in and blew out the candle, leaving me in the dark. No matter. I felt my way off the bed. I put on my shoes and stockings, limped softly to the door, and opened it a crack.

Lamb was asleep, but at the small noise I made, he came awake and unfolded himself sufficiently to make a move toward me. Silently I closed the door again and leaned against it, listening.

My eyes were becoming accustomed to the dark, and I could see the outline of the gaping square of window. Though I yearned to rush to it, climb through and avail myself of the sudden freedom, I made myself wait till I was convinced Lamb had again fallen into sleep, then climbed on the bed.

The words my aunt Minnie had chanted tonight tolled like a dirge in my brain.

Lighten our darkness, we beseech Thee, O Lord; and by Thy great mercy defend us from all perils and dangers of this night.

CHAPTER TWELVE

THE WINDOW WAS SMALL. Shards of glass adhered to the crumbling wooden surround. Outside, just beyond my arm's reach, I saw the moving tree branch, leafless, skeletal. I had planned on stretching, catching hold of it, somehow lowering myself down. But there was that infernal gap between my hand and the limb.

Carefully I picked the points of glass from the bottom of the broken window and tossed them down to the outside ground, then lay flat on my stomach. I squeezed out as far as I dared, the heavy jersey saving me from splinters and wicked glass shards.

"Come closer," I silently begged the branch. "I need you."

Wind plucked at me, hurled my hair across my face, threatened to cast me away, but I stretched myself so I almost tumbled to the ground below and caught the branch. I stretched farther, though that seemed impossible, managed to get both hands around it, and pulled myself out. There I hung, suspended, my hands in danger of slipping on the scaly limb. Dark pressed in on me. I had thought I could wend myself across to the tree trunk and climb down it, but I could see that would be impossible. The branch I clung to swayed and dipped. Between it and the tree trunk was a confusion of other branches and the silhouette of sharp twigs. I was not sufficiently strong or agile to climb through all of them and reach the trunk. How far below me was the ground? Already my wrists were aching with the strain of my weight on them. I had to let go, drop myself into the blackness.

By Thy great mercy . . .

I opened my hands and crashed down.

Instinctively I tried to favor my sore ankle, landing jarringly, my left foot and leg taking the brunt of it. I was drenched both by the falling rain and the wet grass I had tumbled into, but I was there, and comparatively unhurt.

A splinter of glass was embedded in my hand. I felt for it and found it large enough to grasp and remove.

There was the pungent smell of wet manure that the horses had left behind. Below me the great swelling blackness of the sea churned on the sand and shingle. Way out, almost where angry sky met angry sea, I saw lights. Was it a ship sailing in the storm? God help those on it if that was so. Or were those lights from lanterns carried on the boats of my uncle and his associates? Did they launch their boats to help a ship they knew to be in distress? Was this the prize that Angus MacCormick had told them about? Were they to guide it to safe harbor and hope for a rich reward? But nothing in the tone of the voices I'd overheard fitted with that thought. Their words had not been righteous.

For a moment, the unreality of the night consumed me. How could I, Josie Ferguson of 133 Victoria Street, Edinburgh, be here, with a limitless sea below me and a sky filled with storm? How could everything familiar to me have disappeared? How could I be a witness to something I deemed suspicious, even ominous?

I held to the railing of the path so I would not be hurled away. My eyes were accommodating somewhat to the gloom, and I saw people, forty or more, massed on the strip of shingle. The white frills of depleted surf gleamed, almost fluorescent, at their feet. What was their business on the beach on a night such as this? Were they simply drawn to what they thought an exciting happening? Was Eli Stuart among them? I thought not. Some shameful instinct told me that I could have picked him out in a crowd twice this big on a night twice this black.

I saw the horses, still hitched to the carts, high on the dry sand. This was where the men had taken them.

Far out on the sea, the lights of the ship vanished, reappeared, vanished, reappeared as if the sea sucked the vessel down then threw it up again.

On the cliff's edge farther along the Point, I became aware of another light, bright and friendly, swaying along the edge of the bluff.

I rubbed the rain from my eyes. What was I seeing?

Then, like black moths on a black sea, the four fishing boats came into view. They were heading toward the ship that I could see was in great distress. From where I was, the boats looked so small, only shadows that tossed and churned on the boiling sea. If only they were going to save the passengers on the sinking ship. But a terrible disbelief filled my mind. I knew, without any substantiation, that they were going out to the ship for another purpose, though I could not fathom what it might be.

Below on the beach, the crowd stood motionless. Rain pelted them. Spray rose in a mist around them.

Still they stood.

Still I stood.

The world seemed hushed, holding its breath, and then a giant cheer erupted.

What . . . ?

I limped farther down the path and stared out across the sea.

The ship's lights still glowed, but were there fewer of them? Did they tilt low at the stern, high and motionless at the bow, as if resting on something solid?

It was then I remembered that the Sisters were located somewhere there, that long line of rocks, covered now by the fierceness of the high tide.

Wasn't there a warning buoy or bell? Something to show the danger? I had heard nothing. The ship had hit them and in all likelihood was sinking.

"Oh, help them," I shouted, my scream blown back on the wind.

"Hurry in the boats! They are sinking!"

There was new cheering now on the beach. Had one of the boats already reached the foundering ship?

Lanterns flared below, and by their light, I saw dark figures running back and forth, ankle deep in the surf, stumbling out again. Even from this distance, I could see the merriment, the delight. They were shapes in a magic lantern show, strange and sinister. There were women among them. A few. The hems of their skirts dragged heavy with salt water and sand. Their shawls trailed, forgotten, behind them.

A small flame flickered on the sand; the wind caught it and it became a fire and then a bonfire, bright tongues shooting into the sky. Flames and sparks and smoke billowed outward, and the magic lantern figures pranced and danced, alone or with another.

I was bewildered.

But then I wasn't.

What I was witnessing needed no further interpretation.

I could no longer deceive myself.

They were happy. They had hoped the ship would wreck, and now their hopes were realized. And what of the fishing boats, hurrying toward the wreck? They were not there to save but to pillage.

Up on the bluff, the small light I'd earlier noticed had ceased to move. A lantern was held aloft, its yellow beacon moving in circles, which elicited fresh cheers. I realized

that light had been shining for a reason, and it had suc-
ceeded. It was in direct line with the Sisters and could be
mistaken for a safe harbor light. It was not by bad chance
that the ship had hit the rocks. It had been lured onto them.
By a light bound fast to Dobbin's tail as he was led along the
cliff's edge. I remembered the conversation I'd overheard.
Are we takin' Nag this night, Caleb?

My heart was a painful lump in my chest. Such wickedness! Such fiendish arrangements. And my aunt and uncle
were engaged in it all.

A man below had plunged into the surf, waist deep,
a wave catching him and tossing him up like a seal, tum-
bling him over and over onto the sand. He held something
above his head. A chair. Others rushed in then, wad-
ing fully clothed into the surging water, fighting among
themselves, the great rollers smashing them down, carrying them in to toss them on the shingle. Some of those
who staggered back out were empty-handed. Some carried mysterious objects, only a few recognizable: a round
life belt, a crate, a plank of wood. Two men jostled with
a trunk, the surf seizing it, taking it from them while
they struggled to get it back.

These were the treasures they had come for, the God-
sent riches, brought in from the death of a ship. Taken

by the sea from those who had drowned out there on the rocks and brought to the greedy watchers from a ship that had been lured to its destruction.

My hand clutched the railing so tightly that I could not feel it. I was shuddering, and though I gritted my teeth and hunched my shoulders, I could not seem to calm myself.

There was chaos as more and more objects washed in.

Two women scuffled over something, tugging it between them. Was one of them Mrs. Kitteridge?

I closed my eyes. I had become a spectator of avarice such as I had never imagined. Did they give no thought to the poor souls struggling or drowning out there on the sea?

I could no longer watch. But I could not look away.

And then, while my mind grappled with what I was seeing, something else came plunging in on a wave.

I pressed my hands against my cheeks and tightened my body.

No, no, no.

It was a man, lying now at the edge of the sand, waves hissing around him.

Soon I couldn't see him because he was surrounded and hidden by the crowd.

Then I did.

Someone had removed his coat and was waving it like

a flag in the air. Someone else tossed a boot over the heads and onto the high sand.

They were robbing him! Was he alive or dead?

I could stand it no longer. With no thought of what I could accomplish, I was limping, running, and shouting down the path toward the multitude below.

CHAPTER THIRTEEN

A HAND SEIZED MY ARM and pulled me off the path onto the scrub grass and nettles that covered the cliff.

"No," Eli Stuart said. "Do not go farther. You will be in danger."

I struggled against him. "Let me go!" I kicked at him and tried to wrench myself from his grip. "They are—"

"I know what they are doing. But you cannot aid the sailor. He is beyond help," Eli said.

"I don't care . . ." Tears, rain, wind, muffled my words. "I have to."

"No." He was pulling me back, dragging me up the incline, my feet slipping in the wet earth and grass, small stones rattling down at every burdensome step.

I twisted around so I could glance again at the beach.

The body of the man lay inert on the sand. The crowd had finished with him. They were back, waist deep in the sea. The bonfire had been replenished, and by its light, I saw his bare feet, both boots and socks gone, his only clothing now underdrawers and a ragged shirt. He had a beard, black against the dead whiteness of his face.

I could not contain the whimper that spilled from my throat.

"They have not noticed you or us," Eli said. "They are too intent on their business." His voice was sharp, but it gentled when he put his arm around me and helped me to the top of the cliff. "Not far now, Josie."

I could see Raven's Roost. One of the horses on the beach whinnied. I remembered the carts that were hitched to them and knew now why they had been brought.

Instinctively I glanced back at Dobbin's enclosure. It was empty. He had been taken by Bruce, on my uncle's orders.

Eli interpreted my glance.

"The horse has played his part tonight, if unwittingly," he said. "He had a lantern—"

"Tied tight to his tail with a fisherman's knot," I finished.

"Aye. It's a practice that has worked for them before."

"You've never tried to smash the lantern? Or pull it off his tail before it is too late?"

"Aye," Eli said. "I saved two ships that way. But I've been told to wait."

"Who told you? My uncle? Who?"

"Others," he said.

I pounded on his arm. "What others? Tell me!"

But he did not speak. Instead he stopped at the shed. It was closed, but the chain and heavy lock hung loose to the ground. Eli let go of me and pushed open the door, guiding me through.

There was only blackness inside, and I stood, dazed and blind. Then I heard a hiss and blinked in the sudden glow of the lantern that he lighted.

The storm battered the walls and roof. I stared around, at first in bewilderment and then with under-standing. This shed was where the stolen goods were stored. It was a miniature Jackdaws, filled with chairs and oaken chests and ornaments of all kinds. There were pictures in frames, pictures of woodland scenes or farm-lands or the sea in sunlight.

I tried to take it all in, but I was shuddering and my stomach was so distressed, I felt I would surely vomit.

I reached out for Eli, my hands almost touching him

and then his arms were tight around me, my chest pressed against his.

It was just a moment till he let go.

"I thought you were about to fall," he said hoarsely. "These souvenirs have yet to be sold," he added. "To Jackdaws. Or in secret to those who come to buy from far and near."

I recovered my senses.

"They are monsters," I moaned.

We were both soaked. For the first time, I saw that he had on a coarse jacket, roughly sewn. His hair was slicked against his head, and this close, I saw how rain beaded his eyelashes.

"He was alive, and they let him die," I whispered. "They could have comforted him, made him warm, talked —"

"I know. I know." It was like the voice of my mother, kind and gentle.

"Maybe, when he felt land under him, he thought he was saved . . ."

Tears choked me.

Eli reached out across the small space between us and ran his hand across my cheek. And there, in that den of thieves and murderers, where I was still shaking from what I had witnessed down on the beach, I felt his hand on my skin, and a tremor rippled through my body that was from his touch and not from the horror that had convulsed me earlier. Was I losing my reason?

"We must get you into the house" he said, stepping back. "You must change from those wet clothes, or you will sicken."

His words were so commonplace that I was mortified. How could I have felt as I did? At a time like this? I was a disgusting creature, allowing my foolish feelings to obscure, for a few moments, the horror of the night.

"Illness seldom comes near me," I said, in a tone as level as his own. "But perhaps it would be best." I paused. "Lamb, though, is still on guard outside my room."

Eli shrugged. "No matter. I will take care of him. How did you pass him earlier?"

"I broke a window."

He nodded, extinguished the lantern, and closed the door of the shed behind us.

"The ghost of the man on the beach will haunt them," I murmured. "He will not rest."

"I believe you are right," Eli said.

The fire was out in the sitting room, and the place had an air of gloom and damp. It smelled of ale and unwashed men and wet clothing.

Empty jars and jugs littered the table, and the chairs

were spread untidily around the room. This was where the planning had been done earlier. This was where they had accepted me to be part of their villainy sometime soon. It had been my father's wish that I come here and remain here. But he had no understanding of the fiendish ways of his brother.

"I am not sure what Lamb will make of it, seeing me outside the room he is guarding," I said. "Perhaps you will come and ask him politely to move so I can enter my chamber?" I was proud of my well-mannered voice.

Eli would never know how he had troubled my heart, there in the shed.

He went ahead of me up the staircase. Lamb rose as we reached the top step, saw me, leaped forward, and stopped. His demeanor changed in an instant.

"Come with me, Lamb," Eli said, and Lamb belly-slid over to him, a strange submissive moan coming from his throat. Eli turned and went down the stairs, Lamb sidling behind him with drooping head and trailing tail.

What strange power did Eli have over the devil dog? What strange power did he have over me?

The gale screamed in through the empty window space. The corner of the bed with the flowered quilt was soaked from the earlier rain. My aunt had not made it. Some hand, now lifeless, had sewn it, and I had rested beneath it. I discarded the trousers I had bought in Jackdaws and the heavy jersey my aunt had given me. They lay in a sodden pile. Had they come off the bodies of young men, dead and dying? I rubbed my hands along my legs and my body, as if rubbing could remove the horror I felt. The wrapping on my ankle was sodden, the ends of it trailing. I peeled it off.

My hair dripped water, and I dried it as well as I was able and fanned it across my shoulders. It was a style that I had always known to be becoming to me. Eli Stuart was below. That was not what made me comb my hair in an attractive manner, I told myself sternly. I could surely not be so shallow. It was merely so it would dry more readily. Garbed in one of my own innocent dresses and my warm shawl, I went down again to the sitting room.

Lamb was nowhere in sight.

In answer to my unspoken question, Eli said, "Do not fear. I have locked him in the storage room." He had started a fire in the hearth. His discarded coat hung on the banister, and I saw that he was still clothed in the strange skimp of a shirt he had worn the day before, the half trousers. The look of him unsettled me. Embarrassed, I asked, "Are you not cold?"

"I do not feel cold. My grandmother made this coat for me. I wear it only to humor her."

The silver candlestick that we had prayed beside shone

on the table. My aunt and uncle had closed their eyes, invoked God, and then set out to rob and murder.

I positioned myself close to the fire's warmth. "My aunt and uncle and the other men on the boats," I began. "Am I right in believing that they were robbing from the ship, even as those on board drowned?"

"Yes," Eli said.

In my turmoil, I had reached my hands too far into the flames. Eli said, "Have a care, Josie," and snatched them out. "Are you burned?"

I shook my head and stood submissively as he examined my palms, turned them over, his head bent above them. His hair, wet as my own, was polished by the firelight! I had to resist my shameful desire to touch it.

He released me and motioned to a chair that he had pulled close to the warmth.

I could not sit.

"They strip everything and everyone from a foundering ship, should he be dead or alive. If he is alive, 'twill not be for long!"

"But there must be a constable in Brindle. And there's a mayor. Can't they put a stop to it?" I shivered and took a step closer to the fire.

"I informed Constable McBride of the murders that took place on the beach of Brindle Point. I told him how the ships were attracted onto the rocks. He ignored me. Constable McBride was dancing around the bonfire tonight. And they say the mayor's house is furnished like a castle."

"Surely the people of Brindle and the other townlands would report such a crime."

"There's not a one doesn't profit from the wrecking. Any that don't are afraid of the gaffer. Your uncle. He is the boss."

I limped around the room, unable to stand still and listen.

"The Sisters make it easy for them," Eli said. "If a ship in a storm is on a course to miss the rocks, the wreckers make sure it doesn't. There was once a warning buoy that clanged, night and day. Somehow it got dismantled. When it is fixed, it becomes silent again. There are beacons that promise safety but instead attract ships to their deaths. And then there is Nag!"

I stopped pacing to stare at him. "Why did you not tell me this before?"

He shrugged. "I did not know you."

"Huh! You thought I might become party to this wickedness?" Anger flared up, but I had not strength enough to sustain it. I shook my head. "I cannot stay here tonight, not in this house. I could not thole it. I must get away. I must get away forever." I heard my voice rising and could not stop it.

"Yes. But I have to ask you not to go tonight. Not in the dark and the storm. And there are other dangers. Please stay till tomorrow. There are things you must know and do, before you leave. We need you."

"We? You are speaking of you and your grandmother?"

"Do not ask me. Just come. You will be safe. And you will understand everything. I promise."

"If it will allow me to understand everything, then I suppose I should remain till tomorrow," I said.

He had not said that he would miss me if I left forever. He had not mentioned the days after tomorrow.

He did not care.

So be it.

CHAPTER FOURTEEN

WE LEFT LAMB locked in the storage room where I had found the saddle for Dobbin the day I rode into Brindle. Eli filled a bowl with water and set it inside the door. Whatever words he spoke to the dog I could not hear.

We struggled toward his grandmother's house. The rain had ceased, but the storm blew mightily off the ocean, whipping my shawl around me, tossing my hair across my face.

"Wait," Eli shouted, then removed his coarse jacket

and fastened it across my shoulders, letting my shawl drag below it.

"You will be cold," I shouted.

"I do not feel the cold."

"I had forgotten," I said, and did not protest further.

Below us on the beach the good people of Brindle Point and Brindle itself struggled to add to the piles of what had come to them from the sunken ship. There were two drowned bodies now on the sand. I could only bear to glance once, but I thought that one might be a woman. Out where the Sisters hid themselves beneath the sea, were the dark remains of the vessel that had been lured onto the rocks, and I saw two small boats chopping through waves that were big as houses. They were halfway to the shore, heavily burdened, and I pointed and shouted to Eli, "If only they were saving——" but before I could finish the words, I saw two shadow figures weaving up the path from the beach. I squinted, straining to see. One was a woman holding a lantern, her skirt wet and heavy with sand; the other was a child. I gasped. Someone had taken her child down into the midst of that horror.

As the two came closer, I saw that it was Mrs. Kitteridge. She called Eli's name. "Eli Stuart! Eli Stuart, is that you? Will you help me with Daphne?"

Daphne? It was she who had been pining for Eli and whose mother had implored him to come again to visit her. She must be behind them. I made an effort to see through the darkness. Where was she? Had she fallen? But I saw only blackness.

"I think they need my help," Eli shouted to me. "Can you stand alone for a minute, Josie?"

I nodded, though it was likely he would not see such a small tilt of my head.

I watched as he forced himself against the wind and took hold of the child's arm, helping her the last few steps to the top of the path.

"Can you stand, Daphne?" he asked her.

I caught my breath. Daphne *was* the child, a small block of a shape who came no higher than her mother's waist. But her mother had said she was seventeen! Did she mean seven?

"Thank ye, Eli," Mrs. Kitteridge called. "I will be obliged if you will help me get her home. She wanted . . . to come. It fatigued her."

"Are you crazed, taking her down there?" Eli's arm was around the small figure, pulling her with him.

"She wanted to come," Mrs. Kitteridge shouted, and I recalled the way she had bought the dress and slippers in Jackdaws for Daphne. The way she had said, *I can never deny that girl anything she desires.* And then Esmeralda, almost smirking, had said, *Even Eli Stuart?* She'd added, nodding at the dress, *You'll need to shorten it.*

That dress and those slippers for this child?

"Who is that with you?" her mother shouted now in my direction. "Is it Josie Ferguson?"

"Yes," I called.

I took little Daphne's other arm, and Eli and I, together, lifted her to the top of the path.

"Thank you," Mrs. Kitteridge gasped. "Will you carry her home, Eli? I fear she is spent."

"Carry me! Carry me, Eli!" the child shouted, and Eli swept her up the way he had swept me up just yesterday, down on the beach.

I was sore perplexed. My imaginings of Daphne had not been of a child. But nothing in these last few days had been what I'd thought it to be.

Mrs. Kitteridge went ahead, holding the lantern high. The light went out and left us in darkness. The three of us made our slow walk among the storm-whipped trees that shook their branches, showering us with the icy raindrops they'd held concealed.

It seemed a long way, a nightmare journey, Eli carrying the child, who sometimes called out his name as if she could not get enough of it.

"Here we are," Mrs. Kitteridge shouted at last, stopping in front of us to open the door of a dark, square house.

She relit the lantern, and we set Daphne down.

I stared, stupefied. She was not a child but a young woman in a child's small body. Long, fair ringlets hung down her back, so at first sight she appeared youthful. But then I saw her face. It was not the face of a young person. I was stunned and perhaps stared a second too long. She staggered and would have fallen if I had not caught her. "Are you feeling poorly? Can I help you further?" I asked.

She had neither desire to answer me or look at me. Her wide eyes were fixed on him, her hands searched for his.

"She'll be well now." Mrs. Kitteridge shrugged off the cape she wore and divested Daphne of her long, dark coat. Her daughter stood passively as her mother unwound a gray muffler from around her neck, and I saw that she had bosoms under her gray bodice.

"There," Mrs. Kitteridge said.

"See what I found?" Daphne asked, her rapt gaze still on Eli. From a pocket in her dark skirt, she produced a small ornament, a white dog that I took to be porcelain. She held it up. "The sea gave it to me."

I swallowed hard. In an attempt to bring some normalcy to the moment, I asked, in what I took to be a natural voice, "Do you have a real dog of your own, Daphne?"

"No." She bent her head over the ornament, admiring it. "We don't have dogs or cats in Brindle Point. Lamb does not allow it." She smiled up at me. Her teeth were small, like tiny seeds. "The sea is nice. It gave me my dog, and it gave Mama another ring. Show Eli your ring, Mama."

Mrs. Kitteridge held out her hand and displayed a hand now free of rings save for one. The jewel in it was a pearl that gleamed translucent in the lantern light.

"Mama had to cut it off the dead lady," Daphne said proudly. "Isn't it pretty?" She was vivacious now, all signs of exhaustion gone.

Sickness rose in my throat. The pearl ring. That woman on the beach.

Mrs. Kitteridge was turning the ring this way and that on her finger, eyes half closed as she admired it.

"We must go," Eli said stiffly.

"Oh, stay, Eli. Stay!"

I could not bear to see the way Daphne clung to his legs, the way she begged.

I turned my back, not wanting to look further.

"We can't stay, Daphne." There was so much tenderness in his voice that I felt it no wonder that Daphne loved him. I could tell she did.

"Who are *you?*" Daphne suddenly asked of me, as if she had noticed my presence for the first time.

"I am Josie," I said. "I am Eli's friend."

"Are you his sweetheart?"

"No," I said. "Just his friend."

"I am his sweetheart," she said.

He was gently disengaging her hands from the knees of his wet trousers. "We are leaving now, Daphne," he said.

"Will you come again and see me?" Daphne wailed.

"He will. Of course he will." That was Mrs. Kitteridge, soothing and reassuring.

We pushed the door open and were out with it closed behind us. I plugged my ears with my fingers, because even through the roar of the blowing gale, I could still hear Daphne screaming.

"Eli! Eli! Eli!"

CHAPTER FIFTEEN

W

E STRUGGLED ON.

It was impossible to talk. It was difficult even to breathe with the wind against us.

My thoughts surged round in my head. They were too many to sort out. The picked-over bones of the boat out on the Sisters. The ghouls on the beach. The two dead bodies, one the woman who had perhaps had her ring cut from her finger. And Daphne! I could not suppress the groan that came from my lips, and Eli stopped and turned me toward him. "Are you faint? Should we pause?"

"No," I shouted. "I am troubled. That is all."

I was unsure if he heard with the wild turmoil around us, but he nodded, and we began again to walk. I walked with shame, aware of my nearness to Eli. Too aware. How could I be so conscious of him in the midst of so much horror? I was as foolish as poor little Daphne.

Now and then, I glanced secretly at him.

At last he shouted, "Daphne is one of the unfortunates of life. She is not responsible for how she is. Or for her terrible mother."

His grandmother's house arose out of the darkness. Lights in the windows, smoke zigzagging from the chimney, blowing the smell of turf around our heads. All around us, trees bent toward the land, bowing to the gale that blew from the sea. There was a sudden sweep of lightning across the sky. Together we staggered up the shell-lined path to the door.

Before Eli could knock or call out, his grandmother opened it.

"Come! Come!" she shouted, waving us inside.

The glow of the lantern, the heat, and the quiet crumpled me. I would have fallen if she had not supported me, leading me to a seat by the fire. "Dear child," she said. Her questioning eyes found Eli's.

"She has had a shock. And the depravity she has seen has filled her mind —" he began.

I interrupted. "I plan on getting away from Raven's Roost, Mrs. Stuart. I would be obliged if I may stay here till morning."

"Of course, my dear."

His grandmother was relieving me of Eli's coat and of my bedraggled, dripping shawl.

He stood by the door, rain pooling around his feet.

Mrs. Stuart glanced at him. "You must go out again?"

"Yes." He came across to where I sat. "Do not vex yourself more about what you saw tonight. I am only sorry that you did. But it will help you grasp our terrible decision."

"Grasp what? What terrible decision?"

I looked up at him. The half shirt clung to him. His bare shoulders shone, wet with rain. A feeling stronger than any I'd ever had swept over me. If only he would bend and kiss my cheek or murmur a word of endearment! He would not. There was no need to delude myself.

"Why do you always speak to me in conundrums?" I asked him in as angry a voice as I could muster. "Do you think me such a weakling, so mollycoddled that you cannot speak forthrightly? If you have devised a plan to stop this evil, why do you not tell me? Am I not to help?"

I sensed Mrs. Stuart standing very still.

"I do not believe you to be weak. I can only assure you that if I could tell you more, I would. But I am forbidden."

"Forbidden!" I looked at Mrs. Stuart, then back at Eli. "There is that word again! Are you authorized by law in some way, some secret business?"

I waited for an answer.

His grandmother seated herself on the edge of a chair. I saw how tightly she gripped the armrests.

"I am authorized. But not by law," Eli said after a long pause.

"Another enigma," I said sourly. It was good to be angry with him. The anger concealed my other, outrageous feelings.

"I must go."

And that was all he said before he went out, coatless, into the fury of the night.

"I will make us both a hot drink," Mrs. Stuart said. Her kindness almost set me to weeping. It was as though she had seen through my rage to the pain inside.

"Do not be grieving, bairn," she whispered. "He follows the rules given to him. He cannot show affection for you, or even friendship."

I stared at her. "Am I to suppose he is forbidden in that respect also? He is forbidden to confide in me? He is forbidden to show affection for me. If indeed he has affection."

"Oh, he has," Mrs. Stuart said. "It is hard for him, Josie."

I stood, trembling. "Is he a priest? A man of the cloth?"

"No."

Another thought came. "Is he already wedded?"

"No, not that either. You must take my word, Josie."

"Is it forbidden to me to ask you questions?"

"No. But realize I may not have the answers you seek. Or I may decline to answer."

I nodded. "The people here cannot abide him. Why do they not banish him from Brindle? I'm told they have tried to kill him. There is something about a 'three.'" I paused.

"They have tried three times," his grandmother said. "But they are racked with superstition. *The Decree of Three. Woe to those who pay no heed.* The old Brindle superstition they hold to be true. Try three times to kill, and if you do not succeed, it is not sanctioned. His spirit is not ready to leave his body."

I shook my head. "They believe that?"

"Oh, yes. Francis Mulderry scoffed and tried a fourth time. He pushed Eli over Carver's Cliff. But Eli came to a stop in a whin brush and was unhurt."

"And the man? Francis Mulderry?"

"The cliff crumbled, and he crumbled with it. He broke his neck."

Mrs. Stuart's tone was matter-of-fact, and all the time she spoke, she busied herself, stoking the fire, filling a kettle with water, and setting it on the stove.

A coldness moved across me. "But you do not give the saying credence?" I whispered.

"Perhaps I do. Old Brody Leech shot at Eli with a pistol. It misfired. And when he turned up the muzzle to examine it, it went off and shot him in the face. And then of course there was the drowning."

"They tried to drown him?"

"Oh, yes. It is all enough to make the superstitious believe the Decree of Three. And if 'tis true, my thanks to it, as Eli is still with us." She came briskly across to where I sat. "I am not as superstitious as they, but I believe there are things in life unknown to us. I've experienced them myself. Now, let me have a look at your foot."

"It is better, thank you. Scarcely paining me at all."

She took my dirty, wet foot in her hands and examined it.

"Indeed, you are right. It is well healed. You are a healthy girl."

"And you are a magician," I said. "Thank you. May I ask about Eli's parents? Was it from the influenza? My dear mother and father took ill one week and died the next. Was it . . . ?"

"You must ask Eli," she muttered. "I have already said too much."

I could not abide my thoughts. "Please tell me," I implored. "Do not make it another mystery. You *have* said too much, and now I am left to wonder."

She stood for a moment, silent, then went to the fire, emptied water from the kettle on the hob into a shallow pan, and carried it and a flannel to the table. She was not prepared to tell me more. "You will want to wash," she said. "I will find you dry clothes. Then we will see you to bed. Eli will not be back till morning."

I fought down a rush of disappointment. "It is odd to me that he must go again to watch something that troubles him so much."

"Because he is a recorder," she said.

Before I could remark on that, she said briskly, "You shall have my bed. I will make myself comfortable on the settle by the fire."

So Eli was a recorder! I had much to think about. I took a deep breath. "If he is not to be back, perhaps I could have *his* bed." I was immediately abashed by my quick suggestion and by the way my heart trembled at the thought.

"No. Even I may not go in his room," she said.

"I suppose it is forbidden," I said.

"Yes."

I began to undo the buttons on my dress and waited while she rearranged my wet shawl and Eli's coat closer to the fire.

"I will leave you to your privacy."

I washed my hands and face and had finished drying my feet and legs when she returned.

"Thank you for allowing me to stay," I told her. "And for all your consideration. But I must insist that you have your own bed and allow me to take the settle. I will be warm and comfortable."

She did not protest but took the bellows to the fire, flaring up a quick blaze, then went again and brought a nightgown of her own, a woolen coverlet, and a patchwork quilt. I stared at the quilt.

"I made it," she said. "Do not be uneasy. Nothing here has come from broken ships or dead men. The squares are from garments Eli wore as a child. He had no more need of them."

I ran my hand across the patches of color — red, green, blue as his eyes — and imagined him on the beach gathering shells, searching in tidepools.

I turned my eyes away from her for fear she could read my face as she had done once before, and perhaps she did, because she suddenly folded her arms around me.

"Child, child," she whispered, and when I looked at her, I saw her sadness. "I wish that it were not so."

She brought me a cup of warm milk and a slice of buttered oat cake, waited while I finished and till I lay down on the settle. Tucked me in the way my mother used to do.

"Can you sleep, Josie?" she whispered, and I nodded, though sleep was far from me. She was not to know. "I am nearby," she said. "If you call out, I will hear." She lowered the lantern light so there was only the faint glow from it and the brightness of the fire.

"Good night," she whispered.

I lay in the sparsely furnished room. No relics of shipwrecks. Just handmade furniture, an old-fashioned clock that ticked reassuringly on the mantel, the jars of her potions lined tidily on the table. On a coat tree hung a few garments and a knitted cap.

I lay, listening to the storm battering the house, seeing again in my mind the beach, the bodies rolling in on the giant waves, and I hugged the quilt around me for comfort. It was a part of Eli's past. The only part I had of him. Tomorrow, tomorrow I would start back to Edinburgh and put as much distance between me and this vile place as I could. Tomorrow there would be no more Eli. If he had just shown me by a glance or a word that he wanted me to stay longer, I would have. No, I couldn't have. But I would have begged him to come with me. I would have thrown myself upon him. *Stop it!* I told myself. *I will forget him. I have known him for so little time. He is almost a stranger.* But I lied. I knew I would never forget him, that I would yearn for him always.

In the fireplace, the turf shifted, sending up dying sparks. It was growing cold, with the wind searching and finding cracks to smother the heat. There were turf bricks stacked by the fire. I arose from the settle and put four of them on the embers.

Over there, behind the back wall that was within my reach, was Eli's room. I stared at the wall, as if by staring I could see through it. He would not return till morning.

He was a recorder, his grandmother had said. What was he recording? I believed it to be the evil that was happening in Brindle Point. Who was it for? The law? Ship owners who wanted revenge or recompense? Or was he on a quest to find the name of someone who had been killed?

His room might hold the answer. If I knew that, I would know him better.

Entering his room was forbidden. But no one had said it was forbidden to me. I drew a deep breath. I would go in.

—⚬ CHAPTER SIXTEEN ⚬—

I TOOK MY SHAWL from the chair by the fire, then put it back and chose Eli's coat in its stead. It was dry and warm and rough to the touch, long enough on me to reach below my knees. It smelled of the sea and the sun. The lantern, dimmed, was on a hook by the table. I lifted it down and carried it with me as I left the house.

Cold hit me and the wind slapped me back against the door. Just in time, I shielded the flame.

Far out in the blackness that was the sea, the sinking ship looked smaller, the fishing boats deadly toys rising and falling below it. I supposed this would continue till there was nothing left of the ship save its skeleton.

"God help any lives that are still left."

Somewhere, in the shadows, Eli was watching, recording. I wished I knew more. His room might hold the answer.

My lantern gave only a glimmer of light, the globe almost obscured by my outspread hand. "Don't snuff out, don't snuff out."

I stopped, listening to the ragged beat of my heart.

"Curiosity is only prying by another name," my father had told me more than once. "Someday it will lead you where you should not go." This could be a Pandora's box that was said to hold all the evils of the world. If I opened it, would I let the evils escape? Would I ever get them in again?

I shook my head. This was Eli's room, that was all. And he was not evil. I told myself that entering was more than curiosity. This was need, a need to further understand the secret person who had come to mean so much to me.

I had another moment of misgiving as I tried the door handle. What if it was locked? It was not. None of the Brindle inhabitants would try to do him harm or dare intrude on where he lived. In their superstitious minds was ever the Decree of Three.

For better or for worse, I was there, inside Eli's private place with the door closed tight behind me.

I wound up the wick of the lantern and held it high, then stood perplexed, turning my head this way and that.

There was nothing but a table made of two boards laid across two half barrels. A wooden chair. Nothing else? There must be.

I looked around for another door that would lead into a second room. There was none. Where was his bed? His clothes?

On the desk was a book with a red leather cover and a quill standing upright in an ink pot.

That was all. This then was where he inscribed the murderous doings on Brindle Point. To look in it would indeed be prying. I did not hesitate but set the lantern on the desk and opened it.

It was not a story. On the first page was a long list of names.

I sat on the chair and read them one by one.

The first was Caleb Ferguson. My uncle.

Below that, Minnie Ferguson. My aunt.

As I trailed my finger down the long list, names that I now knew jumped out at me.

Esmeralda Davies. The proprietress of Jackdaws.

Clifton McIntyre, the mayor of Brindle.

Mrs. Kitteridge, Daphne's mother. She of the terrifying rings. No Daphne recorded.

Name after name after name.

My trembling fingers turned the page. Another list; all of those names save two were unfamiliar. I knew two. The names of a man and a woman I had never met, but I recognized them immediately I read Eli's words.

Miranda Lee Stuart, 1804 . . . my mother.

Dermott Stuart, 1804 . . . my father. Their ketch, the *Windhover,* lured onto the rocks by false lights.

I was trembling, and the two names seemed to slide away from the page, come back and slide again so that I had to wait and breathe deeply.

This was how his parents had died. Three years since. Poor Eli! Where was he when they drowned? In his grandmother's house? Outside, despairing, watching? Or in some other place, not knowing that he had lost them both?

I forced myself to read on.

Sergio Costello, 1804 . . . on board the *Prudence.* Unknown, 1804. The bell buoy warning muffled by the inhabitants of Brindle Point.

Unknowns . . . off the *Prudence.*

Silas McClintock, 1805 . . . off the *Liverpool Lass.*

Charles Prufrock, aged ten, 1805, off the *Liverpool Lass.*
Maria Prufrock, mother.

On and on. Many Unknowns.

I bade myself to keep reading. Next, in large letters:

Boniface, 1806, eighteen. All drowned. All unknown.

Boniface. This ship's name was on the trunk in Jackdaws
and on my aunt's serviette ring.

The *Sea Urchin.*

I turned the page. There were more. Halfway down the
page, the list stopped. But I felt sure it would start again and
the date would be 1807. Tonight Eli was keeping watch.
He was making a record of the dead. And of the ones
responsible for those deaths. I sat, the wind rattling the
walls, threatening to come in and take me. He had hinted
that those murderers would somehow be punished. Was he
himself going to tend to that? To kill them to avenge the
dead? To punish them for the deaths of his parents?

I drew his coat tight around me. It was cold, cold,
cold. Eli did not feel the cold. I tried to calm myself and

think. What if he were a newsman, writing a story for the *Edinburgh Evening Courant,* the paper my father had read? Or even the *Caledonian Mercury,* to expose this horror? Oh, I hoped that was what it was.

I sat by his desk, knowing that by coming in, breaching his privacy, I had uncovered some things of importance. But I still did not understand. I must be careful if I questioned him, for he must not know I had been meddling.

I slammed the book shut, placed it as it had been, and ran for the door. Outside the storm leaped on me, and I battled it the few steps to his grandmother's door.

It was still warm inside. I draped Eli's coat again over the chair, lowered the wick on the lantern, and hung it back on its hook. The clock ticked, the fire yet burned. I crouched by the heat of it and said a jumbled prayer. So many names, so many deaths, so much evil.

Save me from this place, I thought. *Save me.* I could not think to lie down again on the settle, but I reclaimed Eli's coat from where it hung, put it on over his grandmother's nightgown, pulled his quilt around me, and huddled on the floor by the fire.

I could not sleep. The names from Eli's list slid up and down, endless columns that worried my brain.

Clifton McIntyre.

Mrs. Kitteridge.

The ships. The *Windhover,* the *Boniface.*

Again I imagined Eli, back those three years, watching from the beach as the ship carrying his beloved parents slid off the rocks and into the sea.

Was that how it had been?

The heat from the turf I'd piled on the fire caused me to throw off the quilt.

I had to sleep. I had to have strength for tomorrow, for whatever was to happen.

Sleep, sleep, I told myself, but each command to my mind made me more wakeful.

At last I arose and padded quietly around the room.

I touched the wooden chairs one by one. They were certainly handcrafted. Had Eli made them? I stood by the table, looking at the wooden bowls of herbs and leaves, the small bottles containing different potions that did different things. I picked up the one that held the white sleeping potion.

One hour of sleep to strengthen me for tomorrow.

I held the small bottle to the firelight. The liquid inside was tranquil, innocent as sleep itself. Should I wake Mrs. Stuart and ask if I might have that one drop? Surely she would give it. But what if she said no?

I stood, staring at the bottle, tipping it this way and that so the milky fluid moved inside. It must be safe. Mrs.

Stuart herself had used it now and then. One drop to clear my head of all things horrible. That was all.

There was a sound.

Dear heaven, Mrs. Stuart was stirring! She would see me there, like a common thief! I took a step toward the settle, realized that I still held the bottle, and hastily slipped it into the pocket of Eli's coat.

The sound I had heard came again, a scuffling of feet and then a thump thumping on the door and a loud voice, shouting my name. "Josie Ferguson! Josie Ferguson!"

I knew that hard, angry voice. My uncle Caleb.

The quilt lay in a heap by the fireplace. I took hold of it, wrapped it about me, and crouched behind the settle.

Mrs. Stuart was fully awake. "Who's there?" she called.

"It's my uncle," I whispered.

She made a sign for me to stay quiet.

"Let me in, Missus Stuart, or by my soul, I'll have you in jail!" His roar was louder than the storm's fury, every word filled with rage.

"Go away, Caleb," she shouted back. "'Tis past midnight."

The pummeling and the voice became louder.

"You've got my niece in there. Give her here! I am her rightful guardian."

"Not tonight. She's—"

The lock gave way to a punch or a kick, and in a howl of wind, my uncle burst inside. He wore a long black coat buttoned from collar to hem. Unconfined by a cap, his hair hung in oily strings on his shoulders. He was a demon of darkness, the evil one. I heard the squelch of his boots as he strode toward me. The spots that ringed his ears, those terrible ears, flared crimson.

I stood and held the quilt up before me like a shield, but he tore it from my grip and tossed it on the settle.

Eli's grandmother put herself between us. "Caleb, I will make you a promise. I will bring her to you in the morn. 'Tis a fierce storm, and the lass has endured more of a shock than a body could bear. Let her be!"

"Put on your clothing, girl. You're coming with me."

"I am not—" I began, but he seized hold of my arm and yelled, "You have no need of clothing," and dragged me the way I was, in the nightgown that belonged to Eli's grandmother, in her grandson's coat, out through the broken door, into the night.

CHAPTER SEVENTEEN

I WAS PULLED, HALF RUNNING, half falling, my bare feet scraping the ground.

"Let go of me!" I shouted into the wind.

His grip tightened.

I wrenched my arm free, trying to swing it at his head, but I could not reach and instead hit his chest, which caused him only to imprison my arm beneath his elbow.

Eli! Eli! Where are you?

Below, on the beach, the dark shapes went back and forth, carrying objects I could not identify. The man and woman lay as I'd seen them earlier, stretched out on the sand.

Somewhere, out on some rocks, perhaps on the Sisters, seals were barking.

"I saw!" I shouted at my uncle. "You are a murderer, you and all of them!"

"Hush your mouth!" he yelled. "Not another word!"

He flung open the door of Raven's Roost and thrust me inside with such force that I staggered and fell.

The room was sleet-cold, the fire out. The floor beneath me was a sheet of ice.

And there was my aunt Minnie, gathering empty bottles that clanked and clattered, some rolling away from her on the table, some falling to the floor. It was a scene from an ordinary kitchen, and she could have been an ordinary housewife. She paid no more mind than if I were invisible. I moved to stand, but before I could, Lamb was crouching over me, teeth bared, a growl of fury in his throat.

"Aunt!" I screamed, my scream setting Lamb to snap, his open jaw inches from my face.

"Leave her be, dog," she ordered, and Lamb drew back. "He is angry at you," she said. "He did not relish being locked in the storeroom."

I felt sweat, cold terror sweat, and I edged away from that open maw, sliding sideways like some panicked animal.

"Eli Stuart must have been here," my aunt added. "No one else would dare interfere with my dog."

Lamb lay down on his belly. Was it the very mention of Eli's name that had made him so suddenly submissive?

"Get up, girl!" my uncle said. "Rise and explain yourself."

He shrugged off the heavy coat, and I saw beneath it a thick sailor jersey with the words LIVERPOOL LASS writ large across the chest.

Liverpool Lass! A name from Eli's list.

"I have no need to explain to you," I said. "I do not wish to stay here, in this house of murderers."

My uncle raised a fist, but Aunt Minnie laid a hand on his arm.

"Get upstairs," she ordered me. "Put on some clothing, come back down. We have not finished with you."

"It will ill behoove you to leap from that window again," my uncle said. "It will be Lamb who'll go after you this time."

My aunt stepped around me, paying me no heed. She wore trousers and a heavy jumper, like my uncle's but with no name on it.

I crawled to the chair and pulled myself up, shaking, my legs so weak they could scarce carry me. Mrs. Stuart's nightgown was ripped and dirty along the hem. My feet were bleeding. I limped to the stairs, conscious of the three pairs of eyes watching my progress, my uncle's, my aunt's hard brandy-ball stare, Lamb's green glower, all of them malevolent. Not a one of them had commented on Eli's coat.

I went to my room that was not mine and never would be.

Wind still blew through the window that was empty of glass. My uncle had warned me not to escape through it again, but I knew I could not, even had I so wished. I was drained of energy, my body hurting from the fall on the hard floor, my mind weeping. More than anything, in that moment, I wanted my mother.

I had to get away from there! And I would. I had to clear my head of other thoughts and plan.

I stumbled to the dresser and opened the drawer where I'd placed my purse, containing three sovereigns and eight shillings.

The purse was empty. I groveled around the drawer, searching in every corner, then in every drawer. The money was gone.

For a moment, I was too stunned to think. Then I became filled with outraged anger. They had taken them! There was no one else. Had they taken my mother's brooch? Forgetting my pain, I hurried across to where I'd left it pinned to the neck of my nightgown. It was still there. I unpinned it and took it in my hand. It seemed as if it held all the memories in my world, all the love.

I kissed the pin and set it on the bed, then took off Eli's coat and my nightgown and laid them beside it.

A dry chamise and pantaloons were in the drawer of the dresser, the one below where I had hidden my gold coins. I found stockings that came above my knee.

Hanging on the rail was my woolen dress, green and black plaid, and I put it on. There were pockets in it, tied decorously with drawstrings, and I pinned my brooch inside one, hidden from sight.

My feet were scratched and muddy. I wiped them as best I could before I pulled on my stockings and shoes. Pray Lamb's bite did not get infected again. I took Eli's coat in both hands and buried my face in it. "Eli," I whispered. "Eli." I would not weep. I would not. There was a lump in the pocket. The sleeping potion! I held it and stood still, staring at it. My breath had stopped but my brain was suddenly alert. This potion could be my way out. Depending on how I used it. I would have to be clever. More clever than they were.

I rolled the little bottle that held the potion in my empty kerchief, placed it in the pocket of my dress, and tied the drawstring tight. My mother's brooch was also in that pocket. It seemed an omen. How could I fail?

But for now, I must go down the stairs to face them.

One of them had started a fire. The room had some semblance of orderliness, the chairs back in their places, the empty brandy and ale bottles neatly arranged against the wall. The prayer candlestick stood stately in the center of the table. My aunt was cooking something over the fire. I smelled finnan haddie. My uncle stood, arms folded, his ear growths red as sparks from the fire.

I could not help but stare at them.

His fingers traced the lumps. "You want a closer view?"

I took a step back.

"Everyone gawps at them," he said. "I'm used to it. I was born with them. I'm told that even the midwife who attended my mother at the birth screamed at the sight of them. A sign, she said. A sign of what? I'm an apothecary. I have tried potions, elixirs, even the piss of a donkey that some old woman told me about. I have rubbed and massaged these abominable growths. Once when I was but ten years of age, I took a butcher knife to rid myself of them." His fingers rubbed the lumps, caressing. "Give them a good examination," he hissed. "I sliced the top two off before the blood blinded me."

I forced myself to look. "Yes. I see the two scars," I said as evenly as I could. "I am sorry."

"Aye. Your father was sorry, too. Him with his two good ears on him. He rushed in and wrestled the knife from me afore I could finish. They'd have been all gone by now. It was his fault. All of it his fault. And they praised him. They said he had saved my life, his little brother's life."

I had never heard such venom in a voice. Heat rose in my face.

"How dare you blame him! I am sorry about your disfigurement, but I know that my father purely wanted to stop you from slicing yourself to death. My father had nothing in him but goodness. Have you suspected your deformity might be a forecast of the evil you do?"

I was allowed to go no further. The flat of his hand smacked across my cheek. "Hold your tongue, you besom!" he shouted.

I rubbed my cheek, which had gone numb from the blow, and said, "I look forward to setting the law on you when I go from here."

"Huh!" He moved away, but I heard him murmuring, "Why am I so afflicted? All my life . . ." His muttered words trailed off.

"Food is ready." My aunt lifted the pot off the iron hook that hung over the flames and set it on the hob. It was as if she had not noticed the words between my uncle and me and the way he had slapped me. Or perhaps she did not care.

"Prayers," my uncle said, and motioned for us both to sit.

I held my hand against the welt I felt rising on my cheek and glared at him across the table.

My aunt lit a taper from the fire and lighted the candles.

"Heavenly Father," Uncle Caleb began.

I took a deep breath. No! No! No! God was going to be brought into this. They would pray, the two of them, with blackness in their hearts.

I could not contain myself. "How can you pray? I saw what happened tonight. I saw such wickedness as I had never imagined."

My aunt unrolled her serviette from the *Boniface* ring and placed it delicately in her lap. "You do not understand, but God does," she said giving me a stern look, then closing her eyes and folding her hands in front of her bosom.

My uncle began again to pray.

"Thank You, Lord, for the ongoing harvest of the sea. Thou knowest our needs and suppliest them."

I kept my open gaze fixed on him.

"We ask Your grace in caring for those lost at sea this night," he intoned. "Give our beloved niece, Josephine, the wisdom to—"

I pushed back my chair and stood. Beloved!

"I am leaving Raven's Roost," I said. "As soon as it is light."

My uncle opened his eyes. "That will not be possible."

"It will be more difficult since you stole my sovereigns." I was aware of the nervous tremor in my voice and cleared my throat to hide it.

My aunt spoke without looking up. "We took the sovereigns to keep them safe for you. You are a careless creature, leaving them where robbers could find them. There are thieves hereabouts who can smell gold, be it in another townland."

"I want them back," I said.

"You shall have them two years hence, when your time here is up," my uncle announced. "Till then, you will stay. We have need of the good money your solicitor is to send us each month."

"My father sent me to you, trusting that I would be safe and loved," I said. "He trusted you, his own brother."

My uncle took out his snuffbox, removed a pinch, and this time offered it to my aunt. "Have you considered that I enjoy settling accounts with your father through you? You will stay," he said again.

I waited till they had both indulged in their hearty sneezes.

"Will you tie me up to keep me?" I asked. "For that is what you will have to do."

"If it becomes necessary." His nose twitched in readiness for another sneeze. "Meantime, you will remain seated on that settle till morning, and your aunt will stay with you and keep watch for the rest of the night. I will make decisions the morrow."

"You will go out again on the boat?" my aunt asked him, wiping her nose on her serviette. "Without my help?"

"No. I will be at work on the beach. You must keep both eyes on her, and I will go back about our business. The ship is well under. But there is good substance washing in on every wave, and we'll not be denied it for this whelp of a girl. I'll be there till morning."

Aunt Minnie nodded.

They were speaking openly in front of me now. There was no further need of secrecy.

Aunt Minnie dished up three plates of finnan haddie and set them, steaming, on the table. I had eaten nothing but the oatcake Mrs. Stuart had given me. The smell of the smoked, buttery fish made my stomach lurch. One bite and

I would vomit. But I must eat. I needed to be strong if I was to follow my plan and escape.

My aunt was murmuring words. "My Lamb! You are my Lamb," and I saw that the giant dog was lying by her feet, his big head on her lap. From time to time, she pulled off a morsel of the haddie and fed it to him.

He snuffled contentedly.

"You'll get what's left," she told him.

There was no other sound but the scraping of knives on plates and the gusting of the outside wind.

When we had finished, my uncle nudged back his chair and knelt beside it. My aunt lit the three candles and knelt opposite him. I stayed seated.

"Josie," my uncle barked.

"No," I said. "You may choose to be a hypocrite, but I will not pray in your company."

"Kneel!" he shouted, and before I could gauge his intentions, he rose, kicked my chair back, and forced me to my knees.

I put my fingers in my ears. He could not make me participate further.

Instead of prayers, the words *Help me! Help! Me!* repeated over and over in my mind.

Soon my uncle would leave Raven's Roost and go on with his murderous mission. I did not untie the drawstring on my pocket but surreptitiously fingered the bottle through the heavy flannel of my dress.

When he went, there would be only my aunt left.

My aunt Minnie.

And me.

And Lamb.

CHAPTER EIGHTEEN

H

E WENT.

My aunt set herself by the fire.

"Scrape what's left of the fish into Lamb's bowl," she ordered me. "Wash the dishes and put them away. It's time you put yourself to working around here."

I stood obediently. My mind was on the sleeping potion in my pocket. If I was to get away, now was the time.

Lamb followed me as I went in the kitchen. I scraped the remaining pieces of finnan haddie into his bowl, but secreted the hard skin and the brittle bones in a cup that I set at the back of the highest shelf I could reach.

From the shelf above it, the Toby Jug pirate watched me slyly. *I know what you're up to,* his look said. *You think you can do this?*

Lamb slobbered over the haddie in his dish, then stood up on his hind legs, whining at the high shelf. I realized he could smell the strong, smoky reek of the fish skeleton and bones.

"Come here, Lamb," my aunt called. "Ye had a taste for that haddie, didn't ye, boy! There's none left. Ye must be grateful for what ye got and not be beggin' for more."

The dog ran to her at once.

She bent over, talking to him in whispers.

I poured hot water from the pot on the stove into the basin and began to wash the plates. She was giving Lamb his orders, and I surmised what they would be. He was to guard me should she sleep. He was to guard the door and the window and the stair.

Furtively I watched as he lay down beside her. When I moved, he moved. I wiped the plates dry and stacked them.

My aunt sat upright in the chair. I would have liked to pocket a piece of yesterday's bannock that was wrapped in a scrap of muslin on the counter. It would be food to take with me. But I did not dare. Not with that hard stare of hers that followed my every move.

"If you want to go to the outhouse, go now," she said. "There'll be no leaving this room for what's left of the night."

"I will." Would there be a chance to run once I got outside? What if it was simple as that? It did not matter that it was still dark, that I had no money, that the storm was still roaring. I would go.

Where was Eli? I could not go without saying goodbye. Could I say, "Come for me. Find me! If you share my feelings, if you love me, don't let me go"?

I wiped my hands dry and pushed open the door, feeling the snap of the cold, the slap of the wind. Feeling the heavy beat of my heart.

Lamb came with me.

He lay in front of the outhouse till I had finished and accompanied me back inside. There was no escape. Not yet.

My aunt was where I had left her.

"Reach me the brandy, girl," she ordered. "Sweep the floor, then sit on the settle where I can see you."

I brought the bottle and glass to her. She half filled the tumbler and took a swig, then thrust the bottle at me and nodded toward the table. I carried the bottle back and set it where it had been, then got the whisk and swept as she had ordered. I sat again on the settle, touching the sleeping potion in my pocket.

Which of the two of them should I tend to first?

My aunt! Two or three drops in her brandy. But how would I do it without her seeing?

I waited, planning, my body pulled so tight into itself that my legs cramped and my spine ached.

I thought about how strange it was. I, Josie Ferguson, sheltered, pampered, had found that I could be forceful and daring and brave. Perhaps I had always been, but I had not needed to use those qualities until I had come to Raven's Roost. "Needs must," my father would have said. I took careful heed of my aunt.

At times, her eyes drooped as if she were about to sleep and, when I saw that, I coughed or scraped my feet along the floor.

"You are too noisy, girl," she snapped, and I muttered, "Sorry, Aunt Minnie."

She must not sleep yet. She must be awake and drink of the brandy.

I slid to the edge of the settle, took the little bottle, unstoppered it with my thumb over the lip, and kept it upright inside my coat pocket.

The second I stood she spoke. "Sit, girl! Do not aggravate me again!"

"I am about to stoke the fire, Aunt," I said. "The turf has most burned away."

"Huh," she grunted. "Be quick."

Lamb had arisen, but at the sound of her voice, he lay back down.

With my free hand, I placed two bricks of turf on the smoldering fire.

She was imbibing again, the glass almost empty.

"May I replenish this for you?" I asked. Before she could answer, I took the glass to the dining table and, my back to her, poured brandy from bottle to tumbler.

"Don't be drinking any of it yourself, girl," she said sharply. "I won't have a thief under my roof."

Except you and my uncle, I thought, but did not say. This was not the time to vex her.

I cupped the sleeping draft in my hand and tilted it toward the glass. I was shaking so much that more than I'd intended ran into the brandy. "One drop," Eli's grandmother had told me. I must have used six or more.

But Mrs. Stuart had not imagined this situation. The more the better.

Quickly I swirled the drink around and carried it to Aunt Minnie.

"No need to wheedle at me with your *may I*'s and your sugar-sweet voice," she said sharply. "Leave the glass down and get back on the settle. I mind how impertinent you are. Stay still now!"

I sat.

My thumb was numb from stoppering the bottle, and I eased it away and under cover of my skirt, replaced the cork.

She took a sip of brandy. And another. She smacked her lips.

Her eyes were still open.

Was she never going to fall asleep?

Did the potion not work? What if my uncle Caleb came back? Came roaring in, knocking me senseless, scourging me for my behavior? Waking my aunt, setting Lamb on me?

It was warm in the room, the fire red hot now and crumbling. There was no sound save the wind outside. If my uncle did come, I wouldn't hear him for the storm. I must hurry, get away.

Sleep! Sleep! I silently urged my aunt.

At last her head dropped to her chest. I heard a snore. It could not have been more than a minute since she had drained what was left in her glass, but it seemed an hour.

"Aunt Minnie?" I whispered.

"Aunt Minnie?" Louder.

I stood.

I did not touch my aunt, though I would have liked to

shake her shoulder to make sure that her slumber was deep. But I sensed if I did so, Lamb would jump at my throat. I eased the empty glass from her hand.

After another minute had passed, I went into the kitchen, every nerve tense as I waited for the sound of Lamb rising. The sound came. Then the heavy pad of his feet as he walked after me, the heat of his gaze on the back of my neck.

He did not leap on me. The kitchen must be permitted.

I reached up and took down the cup of skin and bones.

There was panting behind me. He smelled them. He wanted them.

I poured a goodly dram from the little bottle over the fish, set it down, and watched him gulp it away in two mouthfuls. He licked the bowl.

My aunt was slumped over in the chair as if she might fall off, her breathing loud as the bellows she used to gust on the fire.

I kept my eyes on Lamb.

It took him even less time to sleep.

Cautiously I touched him with my toe.

He did not stir.

For a few moments, I stood watching both of them and listening to the howl of the wind in the chimney and the creep of the turf embers.

Then I ran to get a chair. I dragged it under the small, locked cupboard, put my hand into the evil Toby Jug, and pulled out the key.

The lock turned easily. This cupboard had been opened many times.

By the light of the lantern and the glow from the fire, I peered inside.

There was a flour sack tied at the top. When I opened it, I saw the shimmer of gold, coins, medals, a gold chain belt set with red stones, a small silver cup. I picked up the cup. It was heavy, and I saw that there was script on it. With difficulty I read my father's name, DUNCAN FERGUSON, and below it, CHRISTENED THIS DAY OF 3 APRIL 1768.

Tears sprang to my eyes. My uncle Caleb had somehow purloined my father's christening cup. I had been taught not to hate, but it was hate for my uncle that rose, scalding in my throat.

A sound in back of me caused me to start. My uncle?

My aunt, awake?

Lamb?

But it was only a tree branch scraping the wall. Blown by the force of the wind.

I groped farther into the cupboard. There were more coins, a gold chain with a crucifix . . . and something else. Something hard and heavy, wrapped in a cloth.

I pulled it out.

It was a pistol. I understood nothing of pistols but sufficient to know not to point it at myself or anywhere else. I stared at it. Had my uncle killed with this? If he tried to come after me, might he bring this along? Should I take it? The deadly blackness of it, the burnish of the barrels, terrified me. I took a moment to study the mechanism. Was there a bullet in the barrel or the chamber or whatever the shooting part was called? I held the pistol away from me and looked and saw the shine of a bullet. Hastily, before I could think different, I slid the pistol into my pocket. If it went off in there, might it shoot my leg off? I was breathing hard, and the meal of finnan haddie was troubling my stomach. Quickly I extracted three sovereigns from the flour sack. I could not bring myself to take more, though more would surely make my escape easier. In this house of thieves, I would not become one. The pistol was pardonable. Its disappearance would remove it from my murdering uncle.

I dropped the coins and my father's cup into the other pocket along with the sleeping draft, glanced back at the sitting room to make sure my aunt and Lamb were still asleep, then locked the cupboard and dropped the key back in the Toby Jug. The Toby face grinned maliciously at me. *You'll be in trouble. Just wait till Caleb catches up to you.*

He won't! He won't!

I climbed down from the chair so clumsily that I almost fell, then scrambled for the stairs.

In the cold, gusty room, I tied my shawl tightly about me. More than anything I wanted to keep Eli's coat. It was a belonging of his, the only part of him I would ever have. I laid it over the trunk that still held my few possessions and wiped impatiently at the stinging in my eyes. There was no time to waste in being sentimental. My opal brooch was still there, safely pinned. I wrapped myself in my heavy cloak and took one last look around. My bonnet sat perkily on the trunk. I had worn that in another life. It would be only a hindrance to me now. Mrs. Chandler would not approve of a lady leaving the house without it. The white muslin dress hung on its peg, the blue satin dancing slippers below it. Nothing more of my own could I carry, and I wanted nothing that was theirs. Except the pistol! I pulled it out and held it tightly in my hand.

It would have been fitting to slam the door of the room behind me as I left, but instead I closed it quietly. Everything should be quiet till I got away.

The fire was out in the sitting room.

Lamb was stretched at the bottom of the stairs. Perhaps he had been struggling through his sleep to come after me, to do as Aunt Minnie had told him. But the potion had defeated him. His giant body stirred as he breathed. I stepped over him.

My aunt had tipped from the chair and lay sprawled on the floor. For a terrible minute, I thought that I had killed her, but as I watched, frightened, one of her feet moved. I went no closer.

Wind tore at my cloak and almost lifted me from my feet as I pushed through the door of Raven's Roost for what I prayed would be forever.

I stood uncertain. How could I leave without seeing Eli one last time? The words *one last time* echoed over and over in my mind. They must surely be the saddest words in the world.

But how could I stay?

CHAPTER NINETEEN

I T WAS DEEP DARK on the cliff path.

Below me, on the beach, the bonfire still burned, the flames and smoke spiraling skyward. There was no rain to quench it, and its fury turned the air around it a fearsome red.

Where was Eli?

The pistol in my hand disquieted me. I kept its muzzle pointed at the ground. Perhaps I should throw it away? But again, it and its one bullet could save someone, could save me.

The horses on the strand stood passively, their carts piled with wooden sidings and barrels and other merchandise. I saw a long, long piece of rounded wood and knew it to be a mast from the broken ship. They would need a team of horses to carry that.

Would Eli be at his grandmother's house? Going there would delay my escape, but if there was a chance to see him, I had to try. Maybe he would hold me. Maybe he would even say, "I will come with you."

There were three bodies spread out on the shingle now. I turned quickly away, but not before I saw another bundle of clothing come smashing in on the surf. I bit my lips. Was it another body? I did not want to look more, but I was unable to help myself. After one last crash of the wave, I realized that it was indeed a person in the water, alive still and waving his arms.

A man waded into the wave that broke over him. It was my uncle, reaching for the supplicating arm that was stretched toward him. I saw him take that arm, roll the man face-down in the water, and hold his head under while those close to him watched in silence. None tried to stop him.

For a second, I was paralyzed. Then I raised the pistol and fired it, not at my uncle, not at anyone, but above their heads. My ears hurt with the noise, and for a second I was unsteady. But would the shot stop them? Would it save the man in my uncle's grasp?

They were all staring out to sea as if an explosion had occurred in the water. Something off the ship, perhaps.

I closed my eyes, and when I opened them, that fourth body lay next to the others and was already being stripped of its clothing.

The horror of it made bile rise in my throat.

I had wasted the shot. I had wasted time.

With all my might, I threw the pistol as far as I could into the brush behind the path, took the sleeping potion from my pocket, and threw it, too.

Shuddering, I gathered my cloak tight around me and, without another look at the misery below, ran along the path to Eli's grandmother's house. I prayed he was there.

A faint light shone through the window.

No smoke came from the chimney.

I stumbled up the path and banged on the door.

"Mrs. Stuart? Mrs. Stuart, it's Josie."

There was no answer from within.

I tried the door.

It was open.

The room lay cold and empty.

Could she possibly still be abed and asleep through all that was happening?

I called her name, again and again.

"Eli!" I shouted. "Eli!"

Only silence surrounded me, save for the ticking of the clock.

All my senses told me no one was there.

I hastened past the settle where I had slept and raised the wick in the lantern.

The room was tidy, though something in it was different. Her potions and herbs were gone. The table where she'd mixed them was bare.

I ran into her bedchamber. It was empty too, the bed tidy and unslept in.

I must hurry.

I must not miss my chance to get away.

But where was she? Where was Eli?

I ran outside again and into his private room where I'd been before.

There was just the desk where he sat to write. The red leather book with the names inscribed in it was gone.

I stood uncertainly, breathing in the air he had breathed, touching the chair he had sat in, asking myself questions for which I had no answer.

I had to go. No time for wishing or hoping or mourning.

Eli's shells shone, bleached white, as I ran down the

path. I bent and picked one up, touched it to my lips, and slid it into my dress pocket.

I ran, bent over against the gale, through fickle moonlight that came and went at the will of the clouds.

I ran till the pain in my chest bade me slow. The guineas and my father's christening cup banged against one another in my pocket. The shell felt ragged around its rim when I grasped it in my hand. My eyes streamed wind tears.

I walked close to the hedgerows, at times breaking into a run again, ready to slide under cover should my uncle come after me. I saw no one, but there were rustlings in the undergrowth, and I thought or imagined that I glimpsed shadows in the darkness. Once a low black shape darted across the road in front of me. Fox? Or wolf—but I knew from my readings that the last wolf in Scotland had been killed long ago. More likely badger. I felt myself ill in body and mind.

I stumbled without warning onto the main street of Brindle. Every house was dark. No one home. All were on the beach of Brindle Point. One of these shadowy dwellings was Jackdaws. It would have new merchandise for sale very soon.

The sign in front of the Fisherman's Inn slap-slapped against its post. It was a drum, beating out of time.

I was tiring.

My legs and hip ached where my uncle had thrown me to the floor.

However much I tried, my mind refused to stay away from the ship on the rocks, the bodies on the beach, my uncle holding that head under the water, the man's legs kicking, splashing weakly. Would I ever be able to forget?

Alone, at the mercy of the thoughts that jittered through my head, I thought of the past, my parents, their hopes for me. I thought of my aunt and uncle, the blackness of their hearts. I thought about the pistol. I thought about Eli. If only . . . How could it be that I'd met him, loved him, only to lose him? From the beginning, I'd known that he was forbidden. Maybe love doesn't listen to what you know, only to what your heart feels.

Cold seeped through my cloak, through my shawl. Despair was seeping in too. I had started off bravely, filled with determination, but now I doubted. Would I ever make it back to Edinburgh, or would I be found and returned to my "rightful guardian"?

I blew into my hands to warm them, willing myself to take one step to follow the other.

Something loomed on the side of the road. It was a cart, tilted lopsidedly, abandoned.

I approached it warily. Everything, everyone, was a danger.

The cart was old and missing a wheel. I pulled myself into it, so weary I could think of nothing but sleep and an hour of forgetfulness. The cart sides gave me some shelter from the wind and an illusion of safety.

Wrapped in my cloak, I slept.

"Josie? Josie?"

I awoke with a start. Where was I? What was happening? Memory came and, with it, fear.

I'd been found!

I cowered against the side of the cart, then pulled myself up to better face whatever menace stood over me.

And saw Eli.

The surge of joy that came with the sight of him made me forget my pain and despair. I held out my arms, and he lifted me from the cart and held me up, for I would have fallen.

"Is it really you?" I gasped. "Oh, Eli. You came for me! I was sick with sorrow, thinking not to see you ever again. I got away . . . I saw —"

"Shhh! Shhh!"

I buried my face in his shoulder. Through my cloak and my shawl and my other clothes, I could feel the length of him, the Eli strength.

I felt, too, his pulling away.

"How did you find me?" I asked, though indeed I did not care. He had searched for me and found me. That was enough.

"There is only one road from Brindle Point. You had to be on it."

I clung still to his arms.

Wasn't he cold, this cruel, windy, gale-swept night?

I opened my cloak. "You must be frozen. I took your coat. It is back in Raven's Roost. Let me wrap this around us both." I paused. "Oh. I forgot. You do not feel cold."

"I do not." His words were crisp, with nothing in them of affection or wanting.

The realization that I had been leaving seemed insignificant to him.

"You cannot go yet," he said. "When you see the end, you will understand. Come back with me."

"No, I understand enough," I said, though in truth I understood little. "My uncle will find me. He will see how I tricked Aunt Minnie and Lamb. I have told him I will set the law on him when I leave, and he will never let me go. He knows I will bear witness against him." I made my voice as unemotional as his. "I must leave now."

"Your uncle will not be looking for you. He will be

occupied with other things. If you want to help put an end to the murders on Brindle Point, you will come with me," he said.

I tried to see his eyes, but the clouds had again shrouded the moon. "How can I do that?"

"We will tell you. We will keep you safe."

"We? Who is we?"

"Can you just trust me?"

"I cannot trust you. I don't think I even know you. But if you speak the truth, and I can help stop this, then I will go with you."

CHAPTER TWENTY

SOMEWHERE I FOUND the strength to keep pace with him as we hastened along the road that led back to Brindle Point. I could hear my own forced breathing, feel the jabbing pain in my ankle.

He did not ask if I was hurting or too exhausted to continue. When there was sufficient moonlight, I glanced up at him, at the somber set of his face, the grim line of his mouth. What was he thinking? Not of me, certainly. There was an unreality to this night. To everything. Was it possible that I was still the ladylike Josephine Ferguson who had come, unsuspecting, to Raven's Roost not even two days since? That Josie Ferguson who had been safe and cherished since the day she was born?

The wind was still blowing, though not as fiercely. Once there was a savage snorting from the hedgerow. A wild pig? I was too tired to be afraid.

The dark bulk of Raven's Roost rose before us. Were my aunt and Lamb still asleep behind those walls?

Two dark shapes lay on the scrub grass at a distance from the house. I would have tripped over one had it not been that Eli held my arm.

I stared down and gasped.

"Eli! Eli! It's Lamb. And oh." I jerked away from him and bent over the other shadowy figure. "My aunt Minnie."

"Come, Josie! We have no time to linger!"

"But, Eli! Are they dead? Did they crawl out to die? I think I gave them too much sleeping draft."

He leaned over them. "They are not dead. They are still asleep. I brought them from the house."

"Why? Why do I have to always ask you why in everything you do?" I knelt and felt along my aunt Minnie's face. It was cold, her skin smooth and soft. She felt young. I had not touched her before, and she had not touched me in affection or kindness. "Should I get a cover for her? It is so cold, and she wears no shawl or cloak."

There was for a moment the hint of softness in his voice. "Dear, dear Josie. You show no animosity toward one who has treated you so badly."

He moved a strand of my hair from my face to behind my ear. How could just that tremble of a touch fill me with such strange pleasure?

"Your aunt smells so sweetly of brandy that I doubt the cold could even find her," he said. "Time is wasting, and we have none to spare. Already I am late."

"Late for what? You are making me demented . . ."

We were moving fast again, and I had no breath for further questions.

Eli stopped abruptly at the path leading to the beach, and I perforce stopped with him. I stared down at the scene below. Someone had kept the bonfire stoked. The three dead men and one dead woman lay as I had last seen them. Not exactly the same. The woman had been stripped of her green sparkled dress and lay naked, save for her pantaloons and stays. A dark patch surrounded her left hand, and Eli, as if reading my thoughts, said without any emotion, "Sometimes the rings are hard to remove. The sea has bloated the fingers. Best then to take the fingers, too."

Mrs. Kitteridge had benefited.

"Why must they kill those who get ashore?" I whispered. "Is it not enough to rob them?"

"A law was passed. It says if a man or beast is still alive on a wrecked ship, nothing can be taken. They make sure none is left alive, on the ship or on the shore."

I shivered. How could there be such monsters?

Some of the good people of Brindle Point were still jostling with the waves and with each other to snatch whatever the sea offered them, though not much was coming in now. Two men fought over a siding of wood, tugging it between them. Most lay around the fire, spent from their efforts. We could hear laughter and the burst of songs. A hogshead of liquor was being passed in celebration. The smoke, the flames that lit the faces could have been straight from Dante's *Inferno*.

High on the hard sand, the horses stood, perhaps half asleep, their heads drooping, their carts piled high with loot. And with them, head drooping, was little Dobbin.

I saw my uncle. The sight of him sent a wave of nausea through me.

I saw others that I recognized. I saw Esmeralda Davies, the proprietress of Jackdaws; I saw Mrs. Kitteridge. And Daphne.

"She has brought Daphne!" I whispered.

"Look no more, Josie. It is close to the end," Eli said.

His hand on my back ushered me toward the shadow that was his grandmother's house. It was dark, as I had left it. It was not until this moment that I recollected I had left the lantern, still lit, on Eli's desk. It was apparent that we were not going into the dark house but into the bright emptiness of Eli's room. I waited for him to remark on the movement of the lantern, but he did not.

It was cold in there, desolate. Wind whistled around the walls. The sound of revelry on the beach came in spurts like the cawing of rooks. I did not glance at where the red book had been. I was not supposed to know there had ever been one.

I looked at Eli, standing in front of me, splendid as a wild creature, and despised myself for my immediate thought: *How dreadful I must appear with my hair in a tangle, my eyes watering, my clothing dirty and disheveled.* I tried to push back my curls and straighten my cloak so that he would not see me at my worst. As if my appearance were of any consequence on a night such as this. If he witnessed my feeble attempts to improve myself, he did not speak of it.

"There are things I need to say," he said. "I will be leaving tonight, never to return. And you cannot come with me."

I stared at him filled with sudden hope. "Since I am leaving too, can we not go together?"

"Josie!" He took my hand and guided me to the chair by the desk. "No."

"Why?"

"Our ways will be different. I was sent back to Brindle Point for a reason. Now I must return to where I came from. While I was here, I was forbidden to become close with anyone. And then you came."

"I came? You mean, you care for me?" Hope flared in me again. "Who are these people who give you such orders? I want to meet with them. I will talk to them. I will not allow . . ."

He smiled, that smile that trembled my heart. "My Josie," he said. "You are so fierce, and so strong, and so lovely. You cannot meet and talk with them."

"I can. Where are they?"

"Not here."

Tears filled my eyes. "Could you find them for me? I would even beg. I——"

He shook his head. "It is not possible."

I did not feel strong or fierce or even angry anymore. I felt defeated. He was going to leave me.

"Can you kiss me goodbye, then? I would like to have your kiss, just this once. Though I am sure it is forbidden."

"It is," he said, and pulled me toward him.

I forgot everything.

The kiss was the world, and there was nothing else.

Still in the circle of his arms, pressed tightly against

him, I was content. I had not known a kiss could be like that. Surely he would not let me go now? I found myself smiling.

He held me a little away from him.

His face showed no trace of a smile. "It is too late for us, Josie, far too late," he said.

"You are still leaving? You can't."

"I must."

I stared at him.

"You led me to believe that I would help put an end to these murders. That was why I came back with you. Was that a falsehood?"

"It is the truth. I want you to come with me now to where you will be safe. Where you will be able to see and to understand. And perhaps forgive me."

"I will never forgive you," I said. "Never."

In a moment of sanity, I thought, *I know nothing of him. I have never heard him laugh. I have never seen him cry. But I know his kiss. I know he means more to me than anything else in the world. What am I to do?*

He tried to take my hand, but I pulled it away.

I hate him. I love him, I thought. *I will not go with him. I do not want to understand.*

But for the second time that night, I went with him.

CHAPTER TWENTY-ONE

I STOOD ALONE BEHIND the closed gate of Dobbin's empty field where Eli had left me.

The wind pounded me, at times almost knocking me over. There were no sounds now, from the beach or from the cluster of dark houses on Brindle Point. I could have been alone at the edge of the world.

Time passed. I had no way to assess how long I stood there, slapped by the wind, expecting, I did not know what. I relived Eli's kiss. I repeated in my mind the little he'd told me of the night. Leaning against the fence, I drifted in and out of sleep, fatigue winning over trepidation. He had told me I was to play an important part, but here I was, alone, confused.

"Wait," he had said.

I jolted myself awake.

No.

I was not going to remain there not knowing anything.

The gate gave a creaking squeal as I pushed it open.

As fast as I was able, I ran along the cliff path, my body complaining with every step. It wanted dry clothing, rest, heat.

More than that, it wanted Eli.

But he had vanished.

Now and then, a fleeting warmth rose in me as I remembered how he had kissed me. When I thought of his mouth, I shivered. The touch of his hands! He had said I could not be with him. He had said I could not find these others who were keeping us apart. Didn't he know that I would fight for him? That if there was a way, I would find it?

As I hurried past Raven's Roost, I saw that the grassy field where my aunt Minnie and Lamb had lain was empty. Someone had moved them, or they had wakened and moved themselves. I glanced anxiously around but saw no sign of them. There was something in the house that I wanted to retrieve. Something of Eli's.

I steeled myself and went once again into the den of thieves I had sworn never more to enter.

The lantern had burned to a flicker. There was the chair my aunt Minnie had sat in, the glass, empty of brandy, still on the table.

I went quietly upstairs.

The door to my aunt and uncle's bedroom was tight shut. Had it been that way when I left? What if my aunt had managed to come inside and was ready to reach for me? Or worse, if Lamb was in the room?

I cautiously turned the door handle.

No wild barking from Lamb. Only silence. I opened it farther. No one there.

One quick glance was all I took time for. The room was fit for a king, filled with satin pillows, china knickknacks, a mirror held in place by golden cherubs. Who had been drowned to get them? My stomach gave a sick lurch.

No time now for stricken thoughts.

I hurried into my room, took Eli's coat that I'd laid across my trunk, the coat that his grandmother had sewn for him, the coat he had wrapped around my shoulders, threw off my sodden cloak and shawl, and put it on. I would not leave it in this house of the devil.

My gaze fell on the blue slippers that I'd bought, dreaming of us dancing together. Tears sprang to my eyes.

The slippers had been taken from a dead woman. Did I still want them? Yes. I could not abandon my dream.

I slid them into my dress pocket, which was already overfilled, and hastened outside.

But where was Eli?

The moon wandered through masses of cloud.

The night felt biblical. *Yea, though I walk through the valley of the shadow of death . . .* It would not have shocked me if a lightning bolt had opened the sky and struck all the living souls in Brindle Point.

I could not hear the revelers. I imagined them, sprawled around the remains of the bonfire, asleep or still drinking from the jug.

But what if Eli had gone there for reasons of his own?

I stepped to the cliff edge and looked over.

The merrymakers were as I had imagined.

Eli was not there. But my aunt Minnie was. She was conversing with my uncle. In her arms was Lamb.

I bit my lips.

She had wakened, while the dog was still asleep. And she had lifted the weight of him and carried him with her down the path, the way she had carried my heavy trunk that first awful night.

She and my uncle stared up. She pointed.

I stepped back, searching for deeper shadows.

But unexpectedly, a great commotion had started farther along the beach, beyond the cove where I'd seen the fishing boats.

Now those who had been sleeping on the sand had staggered to their feet, gawking, waking one another.

I was gawking too.

The length of the cliff path as far as I could see was filled with dark shapes, moving, marching, all coming this way. A mob, a multitude.

The trail was filled with them, the night loud with their tramping feet. The ones at the back carried lit torches that flared above their heads.

I stood, uncertain, my back pressed against the outside wall of Raven's Roost. Waiting.

CHAPTER TWENTY-TWO

THEY MARCHED TOGETHER two or three abreast. Men, women, children. They did not talk among themselves. I stood, stiff and scared, as the first two passed close to me, never glancing in my direction. Had they come to stop the murders on Brindle Point? How was I to be a part of it?

Farther back, I saw torch carriers. Suddenly there was a flare and then a blaze, and a house was afire. Then another and another. The wind was lifting the flames, hurling them house to house.

Brindle Point was burning.

Smoke rushed toward me. My eyes stung, and I blinked to try to ease them.

Passing me now was a lady in a blue shantung dress. I'd seen that dress before. In Jackdaws. Mrs. Kitteridge had purchased it for Daphne. I looked at the lady's feet. She wore blue satin slippers with beading on top, *my* blue satin slippers.

It couldn't be.

I fumbled in my pocket and pulled out the slippers that I'd placed there just minutes before. "Do not assume dreadful things," I told myself. "Do not. These slippers are similar. They cannot be mine."

Young men, sailor men, twenty or thirty of them in dark trousers, strode along. Who were they? The men wore jerseys with the word BONIFACE writ large across the fronts. And there were more with LIVERPOOL LASS in white letters on their chests. Others, seamen all. Two or three of them wore what Eli wore, the sleeveless singlet, the cutoff trousers. I clamped my hand over my mouth, afraid that I might scream. These sailors were the Unknowns in Eli's list. I was becoming more and more certain of it.

I should run, hide from this unimaginable horror. But I could not. There were gentlemen in ordinary clothing and a few women, two small boys, a man with a child on his shoulders, a woman with a baby wrapped in a shawl. The woman pointed down to the beach at a man standing alone at the edge of the surf. In a strong voice she yelled, "You! You! You would not save my baby, though I begged. Instead you took a roll of wire into your boat! I curse you, you fiend!"

The man she pointed to was the mayor of Brindle. He shrieked, then threw himself face-down on the sand.

There was a marcher, bent over, carrying a violin. There must in the world be many violins, but I knew instantly that this was the one that was displayed in my aunt's living room. And that man with the white face and bushy black beard? I had seen him robbed of all his clothing, lying dead on the beach.

And I saw Eli.

In his hand, tight against his chest, was the book with the red leather cover.

Not Eli! Please, God. Not Eli!

He walked between a man and a woman. She wore a simple white dress, and at her neck a gold chain with a gleaming purple stone. She was the woman in the painting that hung in Mrs. Stuart's house—Eli's mother. His grandmother had said, *That was the dress Miranda wore the night she drowned.*

Every inconceivable thing became a certainty to me.

These were his parents. His parents who had been on board the *Liverpool Lass*. All these marchers were dead, dead at the hands of the people of Brindle and Brindle Point.

Eli's parents were dead.

Eli was dead.

The look of him there with those living corpses destroyed me.

I stifled a scream.

How could he be dead? He'd held me, carried me, kissed me.

I wanted to run to him, but my feet would not move.

He had seen me, and I saw him whisper something to the woman, his mother, then come to where I stood.

I stared at him, speechless.

He ran his hand across the smooth darkness of his hair. The red-leather-covered book was held tight against his chest.

A sob, like a hiccup, racked me. "Tell me," I whispered. "Help me understand. If I can . . . I don't know —"

"Shhh! Shhh!" He stroked my cheek. "I need you to be strong. I was on the *Liverpool Lass* with my parents when it was wrecked on the Sisters. I was working on the sails, helping in the storm. Your uncle and the others believed I had survived. They were wrong. I drowned too."

I shook my head, shook it over and over. "You can't have. If you drowned, you wouldn't be —"

"They thought I was still alive. But they sensed a strangeness. They feared me. They could not kill me."

I was crying, and he held me, whispering into my hair. "Oh, Josie! From the start, I knew there was a line we could not cross. That I should stay away from you. But I could not. I ask your forgiveness."

I looked into his face. "Don't say that. I care nothing for the line. I will break through it. Only take me with you."

"I cannot." He bent, and for a moment, I felt his lips on my brow. "You will go back to Edinburgh —"

"I will not go back. I will follow you into the darkness."

He took his arm from around me and with his thumb wiped away the tears on my face. "No. Do not try to find where I am," he said. "I cannot be found. You will forget me."

"Never! You are speaking to me as if I am a simpleton. I can decide."

"No, my love. On this you cannot." The words were so definitive, his face so anguished.

I tried to hold him.

Beyond where we stood, the fire roared. I saw it licking at the trees around his grandmother's house.

"Your grandmother?" I gasped.

"She is safe. She has been taken to live with her sister in Kilbarchan. Arrangements were made. And I brought your aunt and Lamb from inside Raven's Roost. We want no more deaths on Brindle Point."

The marchers had turned now, walking silently on the road that led to Brindle, their torches flaring ominously into the darkness above.

There was wailing from the beach below. Howls. I paid them no mind.

Eli held out the red book. "You asked how you could help. This is how. I have recorded the names of those who have been murdered. As many as I know. And the names of those who murdered them. Take the book with you. Give it to the authorities. Can you do that for us, Josie?"

I could find no more arguments. "I will do anything you ask."

"Your journey to Edinburgh has been arranged," he said.

"I don't know how. None of this can be happening. Tell me it's a dream, a horrible, horrible dream!"

"It is not."

"Will I ever see you again?"

"Maybe," he said. "In another place."

He lifted my hand, kissed it, and was gone.

CHAPTER TWENTY-THREE

I SANK DOWN ON THE PATH.

The smell of smoke, of burning wood, swamped me. My thoughts were so jumbled, I could not contain them.

There was keening from the beach.

Some of them started up the path, clawing, crawling, pushing one another.

Others called, "Stop! They're still there. They'll set you afire."

"God help us!"

"They're ghosts."

"The dead have risen. Have mercy on us, God! Have mercy!"

Some ran into the sea.

A woman and a man had pulled a plank off a cart and were pushing it through the breakers, clinging to it. They were my aunt Minnie and my uncle Caleb. The dark shape I saw on the plank was Lamb. I watched as a great whitecap smashed down on the wood and tumbled all three of them into the water.

I pulled Eli's coat tight around me and held the book hidden against me.

Let them howl and scream. I had no pity for them. Maybe God would, but I could not.

My mind was in such turmoil.

The fires, the gale, the sight of those men and women and children already dead, had taken away my senses.

Eli was gone from me. I now knew it to be forever.

How was I to go on?

Weariness overcame me. My eyes stung from the bitterness of the smoke.

There, on the cliff, Raven's Roost burning behind me, I was overcome with exhaustion. I closed my eyes.

And that was all.

I T IS NOW ONE YEAR since I was taken from Brindle Point and brought back here, I do not know how. I opened my eyes, and I was here.

I live in our old house. This, along with money for my support, was arranged by my solicitor. The house seems empty without my dear parents, but Mr. Brougham hired a kind woman to stay with me and attend to my needs. He was shocked to learn that my aunt and uncle were the ringleaders of the wreckers of Brindle Point, and that Raven's Roost had been destroyed.

I set down on paper what I had learned in those two days at Brindle Point and gave it to him.

My account detailed what I knew of the wreckers who destroyed ships and murdered the survivors. I told of the huge fire on that dreadful night—the wind that whipped the flames savagely along the trees and hedgerows and consumed everything it touched, not only on the Point but in the town of Brindle. I gave him the book with the red leather cover, where the names of the dead and those who had killed them had been recorded. I said it had been entrusted to me by one of the innocent homeowners. As my solicitor took it from me, a spark jumped from my fingers, sharp enough to make me recoil and gasp. I looked to see if Mr. Brougham had experienced it as well, but he was calm and serious as ever. Afterward I thought that spark had signified the end of the end.

The investigation commenced without delay. Many of the wreckers have been found, scattered around the countryside, and are awaiting trial. My uncle and aunt and Lamb are not among them. Perhaps they drowned. I do not know.

There is no more Brindle or Brindle Point. The only inhabitants are the seagulls and the rooks and ravens that caw in the trees. Folks stay away. It is said that both places are haunted, and they may well be.

I have not told anyone of the avenging angels that marched that night. I have no clear memory of them myself. Sometimes, in my mind, they are people, sometimes real angels with wings carrying burning brands.

I did not tell of Eli.

Eli!

I have tried to pull him back into my mind. I strive to remember his smile, his touch, but he has faded from my memory. I think I remember the blur of a kiss. There is nothing left but his name and a shifting recollection of tenderness.

I have accepted now that there are things in this world I do not understand. Perhaps I am not meant to understand. But I know myself to be stronger than I was. I know I can withstand whatever my life brings. It gives me satisfaction to realize that I helped bring peace to those who drowned and justice to those who caused their deaths.

On the chiffonier by my bed is a shell that must have come from that time. Next to the shell is my father's christening cup, and beside it blue satin slippers that sparkle in the light from my lamp. I stare at these things and try to remember, but I cannot.

Did I dance with him, this shadow person?

Did I love him?

I take the slippers in my hands and decide I will wear

them when I go to the Devonshire Ball with my new beau, James Forsythe. James was introduced to me by Mr. Brougham and immediately I felt drawn to him. He reminds me of someone. James has hair black as a crow, and blue eyes that sometimes change to be almost green, like my mother's opal brooch. He has a way of looking at me, intently, knowingly.

I will dance with him, this person who reminds me of someone else. I will put the past behind me. And I will try to be happy.

WRECKING IS THE PRACTICE of taking valuables from a wrecked ship that has foundered close to shore.

In the nineteenth century wrecking was widespread in the United States, Bermuda, Canada, Great Britain, and many other countries with rugged shorelines.

The Pentland Firth, a stretch of water off the northern coast of Scotland, was well known for its many shipwrecks. At this time, when mariners had no navigational charts and no lighthouses to warn them of hidden dangers below the water's surface, ships were in constant peril. Rocks, fogs, Atlantic gales, and strong currents were responsible for the sinking of many a sailing ship in the Pentland Firth. But there were times when a shipwreck caused by natural hazards was made fatal by wreckers, helping nature along.

On the shore a lamp would be tied to a donkey's tail. The animal was then walked along a cliff's edge or along a beach, the lamp moving up and down with each step the donkey took.

To those on the doomed ship, the lamp shining through the darkness appeared to be the light from another vessel, bobbing in a safe harbor.

The captain would set sail in that direction and be lured onto the jagged rocks close by. "False lights" brought easy pickings to a bunch of greedy wreckers.

The wreckers took whatever they could fit into their own small boats and whatever plunder they could carry off. A small coastal cottage might blossom with a grand piano, or a gilt mirror, or a dining room table. Some of the goods might be sold. Wreckers were not all vicious. Many were just desperately poor, hoping to improve their harsh lives. But the deadly outcome was the same.

A law was passed making it an offense to use false lights to entice a ship onto rocks, but there is no record of anyone being prosecuted. Another law, known as the Man or Beast

Law, stated that nothing could be removed from a wreck if "a man or beast" was still alive on it. In some cases this may have helped keep passengers and crew and even livestock safe. But in other instances it made things worse. Wreckers were not reluctant to kill any person or animal still alive and take the plunder they had come for.

To scare away those who wanted a share of the riches, the wreckers told stories, sworn to be true, of haunted ships and wailing ghosts. Even now, in dark nights on a lonely seashore, phantoms and phantom ships are said to appear out of the sea mists that cloak the Pentland Firth. Other ghosts too, torches flaring, reportedly walk along the cliff path that passes Raven's Roost.

Perhaps they do.